SINCERELY

S.L. ROTTMAN

Published by AFterwords
©2012 S.L. Rottman

Cover designed by Art Wickberg

Summary: Fourteen-year-old Silke Reichard has abided by
her parent's strict code of conduct without much complaint,
but one weekend of freedom shows her that sometimes it's
okay to take chances and break a few rules.

ISBN 978-0-9799812-4-1

Once again with love and gratitude for
my family's understanding and support.
Sincerely

CHAPTER ONE

"Can I come with you instead?"

"Sure," Alexi replied sarcastically. "I know your mom won't care at all if you cut class on the first day of school."

I groaned. Social studies was the one class I had been dreading ever since we had gotten our schedules last week. Alexi and I had English, Spanish, and science together. Mariel and Emma were in my math and PE, and Taylor was in choir with me. Best of all, we all had the same lunch period.

But I didn't know a soul in social studies.

Well, okay, I knew I'd know people in class—after ten years in the same district, you got to know people. Even though this was my first day in high school, I knew people. But they weren't *my* people. They were the cheerleaders or the nerds or the jocks. Not normal people. Not my friends.

"Maybe cutting would be worth it," I said.

"As if you'd dare," she said, rolling her eyes. "We all know you'd never, ever cut class."

"Maybe this year I will."

Alexi paused, regarding me in the crowded hallway. "You think so?"

"You never know," I said, shrugging as if just the thought didn't set my heart racing.

"I know you, Silke. And I know your mom." Alexi was my best friend. She knew how often I had contemplated being bad lately, and she knew how much my mom would freak out. On more than one occasion this summer, Alexi had been the voice of reason, even going so far as to end IMs with me when my allotted hour of computer time was up.

"See you after school," Alexi said as we reached the corner.

She hung a left, blending immediately into the sea of students swarming the hall and leaving me to walk the remaining way alone.

Clutching my notebook to my chest, I hurried past three more doors to room 110 and ducked inside. At least it was the last class of the day. I scuttled to an empty chair by the far wall before I looked around the room.

Mr. Norton was standing behind his desk, talking to a couple students, and they didn't look happy. Neither did he. This was my first class with Mr. Norton, but everyone knew his reputation. Big and burly, even for a football coach, he was said to be fair but strict, and virtually unforgiving if you ever crossed him. From the look of things, there were already two guys who would be scrambling to the counselor's office to beg for a schedule change.

A couple of girls walked into class together and took the two desks in front of me. A few guys came in laughing, one shoving another through the door, but they stopped as soon as they saw the look on Mr. Norton's face. They quickly found seats on the other side of the room, and I sighed with relief. No one was next to or behind me. I knew almost one third of the class by sight, but a lot of kids were either from the other middle schools or had moved here this summer.

Mr. Norton waited at the door, ready to pull it shut as soon as the bell rang. He motioned with his hand, encouraging someone to speed up. In perfect sync with the bell, the newcomer slunk into the room as Mr. Norton closed the door.

Everyone stopped talking, even before the door clicked shut, but no one was watching Mr. Norton. We were watching the new guy. He was gliding, in a slouched over kind of way, across the room in my direction.

His hair was a mess. Not only did it look like he had just woken up, with one side of his hair standing almost straight up, knotted and confused, and the other side matted down on his cheek, but it was a hard color to describe. I reached up and tucked my own extra fine, white-blonde hair behind my ear.

As the stranger got closer to me, Mr. Norton began speaking. I tore my eyes away from the new guy with difficulty.

"Welcome to Western Civilizations," Mr. Norton said, moving next to his computer; at the same time, I felt my desk shift ever so slightly. The new guy was right behind me.

"My name is Mr. Norton, and I teach high school. I teach high school because I don't want to work with small children or immature teenagers who don't know how to think for themselves. I teach high school because I like to work with young adults who have minds of their own and know the meaning of responsibility." His dark eyes swept over the class, and I tried to sit up a little straighter.

I was having a hard time concentrating though, because an overwhelming stench was drifting past my desk, making my eyes water. I didn't think it was cigarette smoke, but it was awful.

"Because I expect you all to be responsible young adults, I will not be giving you a seating chart. You may sit where ever you like," he raised his voice ever so slightly to cover the murmur this announcement caused, "and you will accept the consequences for doing so. If you and your neighbor decide to talk, ladies," he glared at the two girls in front of me and they immediately shut up, "you will face the consequences. The first consequence for talking out of turn is a warning, the second is a zero for the day's work, and the third is detention."

"What's the fourth?" asked one of the guys across the room.

Mr. Norton leveled his stare in that direction, and I didn't blame the guy for sliding down a bit in his chair. "If you are careless enough to cause a fourth disruption in one class, or a third one in a week, you will be sent to the office and be given a day of in-school-suspension."

The class was quiet.

"And after that?" a deep voice drawled behind me. It almost sounded like James Earl Jones was sitting in our class.

Mr. Norton looked in my direction, and I had to remind myself that I was not the one being skewered; the glare was aimed at the guy who hadn't combed his hair.

"That would not be wise."

Mr. Norton continued to stare over my shoulder, and I carefully fixed my gaze on the smart board behind him. After what seemed like a really long time, Mr. Norton resumed.

"Here is an attendance sheet," he said, holding up a blank piece of paper. He handed it to the girl in the desk closest to him. "Sign your name and pass it on."

"Notes are your responsibility. Anything I take the time to write on the board, show in a PowerPoint, or repeat twice, I suggest you write down. Again, notes are your responsibility, and if I write something on the board, show it on a slide or repeat it, it is something you need to know."

Immediately I snapped open my notebook and fished a pen out of my bag. Mr. Norton nodded to me as he turned on the projector, and a few seconds later there was a general shuffling as everyone else in the class got their notebooks out.

Forty minutes later, I thought my hand might fall off from all the writing I had done. I wasn't the only one, because when Mr. Norton turned off his computer, several people sighed with relief.

"Notes, assignments, knowing when quizzes and tests are scheduled, these are all your responsibility," he said, "Your responsibility, not mine. I recommend you take the last five minutes of class and find at least three people to exchange contact information with, because I will not tell you what you missed in class. I further recommend that you exchange information with people who you believe will be able to help you, and not look to your friends. It is my experience that when one friend misses a class, quite often the other one is ditching with them." He smiled. It was the first smile he had given us all hour, and it was rather frightening.

A hand touched my shoulder and I flinched.

"Sorry," the guy said as I turned to look at him. His deep voice didn't match the rest of him. "Didn't mean to scare you."

I tried to smile to show that it was okay.

"Can I get your name and number?"

"Excuse me?"

"In case I miss class," he said, gesturing to the front of the room and Mr. Norton.

"Oh. Yeah. Sure." I scribbled my name and number on paper and handed it to him.

He started writing on the bottom of the page, and I stared at the mass of multi-colored hair. There were streaks of red, blond, blue, brown, orange, black, and green. *Horrible dye job*, I thought. *A rainbow gone amok. It had to be a really bad dye job. No one would ever look like that on purpose.*

"...hair?"

"What?" I felt my face flush as I tore my eyes away from his head.

"Is your name pronounced Silk-ee, like in silky hair?" he repeated, looking up at me. His eyes seemed a shade darker than the strands of green curling around his ear.

"Um, yeah, Silke," I said. "It's German," I added for some reason.

"And you're—" I looked at the half of the page he had handed back to me, "Dominic?"

"Yep. Just a name, though. Doesn't mean anything cool like Silke."

"What's Silke mean?" I asked.

He blinked. "I thought you knew. You know, since it's German, it must mean something special." He tore off the bottom half of the page where he had been writing.

"I don't think so," I said, looking at him strangely.

"Maybe you ought to look it up, check and make sure."

I stared at him. "Excuse me?"

"Well, it doesn't seem smart to be pointing out the fact that it means something else when you don't know what it means. After all, what if it's German for snotty or dirty snow?"

I so desperately wanted to snap at him, but I couldn't think of a single syllable.

"You can text me if you want, let me know what you found

out." When I didn't say anything, he prompted, "Okay?"

"Yeah, sure," I said, taking the paper he was holding out to me and stuffing it into my back pocket. Everyone in class would have to die before I'd text him.

"Hey," one of the girls in front of me said suddenly, "Want to exchange information?"

"Yes!" I said, and when the bell rang, I was so busy talking to my new friends—Bridget and Daisy—that I hardly noticed that Dominic was the first one out the door.

*   *   *

"So how was class?" Alexi asked when I caught up to her in the hallway. "Is Norton as terrifying as you thought?"

I frowned. "I'm not sure. He's definitely got rules that you don't cross, but he's also kinda fun to listen to."

"Fun?"

"Yeah. He's got this sarcastic way of talking—"

"Ah, rules and sarcasm! Two things we know you can handle!" Alexi said with a smile.

"Are you done yet?"

"Is that sarcasm?"

I bumped her with my shoulder and she just laughed.

"Guess who's in painting with me?" She asked with an all-too-innocent expression.

"No way!"

"Way! And guess where he sits?"

"Seriously? Adrian Simmonds sits next to you?"

"Sshhh!" She clamped a hand over my mouth and stared around.

I pulled her hand off. "Oh, please," I said, "Let's pretend everyone at school doesn't know that you've been crushing him since third grade."

"See? Sarcasm."

"It's so unfair," I moaned as we stopped at our lockers.

"What? That I know you better than anyone?"

"That you get Adrian Simmonds and I get…. Argh, why can't I get my lock open on the first try?"

"Because it's the first day of school, nit wit. Who's in Norton's class with you?"

I was gnawing on my bottom lip, trying to get the stupid lock to cooperate—and making Alexi wait in the process.

"Silke! Who's in your class? Is it Jason?"

"No," I snapped. Instinctively I looked over my shoulder, checking to make sure that none of Jason Miller's friends—or worse, Jason himself—was nearby. Adrian made Alexi's heart go pitter-patter when he talked to her; Jason made mine stop just by being in the same room.

No one nearby seemed to be paying any attention to us. I returned to trying to get my lock open. Finally, it popped. I opened the door.

Immediately, Alexi slammed it shut. "Are you going to talk to me or what? Who is in your class?"

"Dominic."

"Dominic?"

"Mm-hmm." I was spinning the lock dial around again.

"Dominic who?"

"I dunno."

"Silke!"

"Honestly, Alexi, I don't—wait a minute," I said suddenly. I reached in my back pocket and pulled out the paper with Dominic's information. "Um, Dominic Martin."

Alexi frowned. "I don't know him."

"Me either."

"Then what are you doing with his name in your back pocket?" she asked, waggling her eyebrows at me.

"Mr. Norton had us get people's name's and numbers so we could call if we miss class or need help."

"Is he cute?"

"Hard to tell," I said, thinking of his deep green eyes and voice and totally insane hair. "He's different."

"Oh?" Alexi popped her locker open and I immediately

slammed it shut, but it didn't matter. Alexi spun the lock around deftly, and popped it right open. "How?"

"He's got about twenty colors of hair."

"Twenty colors? You mean shades?"

"No. I mean colors. Red, blue, yellow, brown, blonde, purple.... twenty different colors. On one head. It's a rainbow gone amok."

Alexi stopped and looked at me. "His hair's about this long?" she asked, holding her hand just below her own shoulder-length red hair.

"Yeah."

"I saw him this morning. Kind of freaky looking."

"Nnn—" I hesitated. "Odd maybe, but not freaky."

"Is he nice?"

"I don't know. I didn't really talk to him. He's kind of—"

"Freaky?"

"Yeah. I guess he's kind of freaky looking."

"'A rainbow gone amok,'" Alexi said, shaking her head. "Sometimes I worry about you, Silke."

"What?"

"Only you would talk that way."

I shrugged. "Ready to head home?"

"Yeah. Let's go."

*   *   *

Alexi lives two streets over from me. In first grade she called me a ghost, and I had cried and said I hated her. In second grade, she punched Reggie Collins in the stomach when he called me liar, and we had been best friends ever since.

"Raquel said the first football game is an away game," Alexi said, "And she thinks her brother might be able to drive us."

"Have fun," I said.

"Aren't you even going to ask if you can go?"

I shook my head.

"She's been getting worse, hasn't she?" Alexi asked softly.

"No, I've just got other things to fight for," I said with a smile.

"Such as?"

"Choir."

"You're in choir because your mother wants you to be in it. You don't have to fight for that."

"Yes, I do," I told her. "We've got an awesome Christmas field trip coming up."

"Going to perform at the mall?"

"I said awesome, not awful! You'll never guess."

"So tell me already," Alexi said.

"New York!"

"That is awesome, but you know you're not going."

"Maybe not," I said, "But at least it's a possibility."

"Ha."

"Way to kill my dream, Lex."

"Sorry. It's just—"

"I know." I sighed. Mom only let me go on field trips if she or Dad were chaperoning, and the chances of either of them having enough time to go to New York with the choir were about none.

We said good-bye at her house and I continued on. Pioneer Elementary was on the street between Alexi's and mine. Every day, I was to be at Grete's school in time to pick her up and walk her home, or face my mother's wrath. When Grete had started kindergarten, Mom had been there for her every day afterschool. But then her seminars started getting really popular and she began travelling a lot. So it fell to me to get Grete safely home every day.

I set my bag down and sat on the curb to wait. Days like this weren't too bad; the sun was out and a light breeze spun the dandelion fuzz down the street. In January, when it was likely to be cloudy and the wind would cut the temperature down below zero, it sucked to wait twenty minutes after school. Sometimes I'd stay at the library, trying to time it out so I wouldn't have to wait more than a couple minutes for her. I had to be careful, though, because if Grete got out before I was there and she waited for me or just started walking home, I got in trouble. It was worth five minutes of freezing to not get grounded.

I pulled my cell phone out of my backpack and turned it on. Technically, we weren't allowed to have them at school, but my mother insisted I keep it with me. Her opinion was that if I kept it off and in my backpack, it wouldn't get me in trouble. If I dared to turn it on during school hours, however, she wouldn't skip a beat before restricting me even more. I was supposed to turn it on as I left school everyday, in case she needed to leave me a message.

I had a message, but it wasn't from Mom.

"Hey, Silke, we're going to go to the mall this weekend. Mariel overheard Adrian saying he's working at the Lickin' Chicken on Saturday. Can you go? Call back!" And Emma's bubbly voice was replaced by a quick beep.

I'll try, I texted back. I'd have to wait until Friday and prove that I had finished all of my homework for the week before I could even ask Mom if I could go.

An excited babble of voices came from the school as the little kids were released. I stood up and waited for Grete. She ran up, golden blond curls bobbing and green skirt swaying.

"Silke!" she cried, "I had the bestest day!"

"Yeah?" I asked, turning to walk with her as she slipped her hand in mine.

"Oh yeah," she nodded. "We've got bunnies!"

"Bunnies?"

"Bunnies and turtles and a rat! Class pets!"

"Really?"

"Uh-huh! And not only that, we get to take care of them."

"Cool."

"And Jilly is in my class too."

"Hooray." Jilly was Grete's best friend. Sometimes it felt like Jilly was a second sister, she was over at our house so much. "How was school?"

"I just told you!"

"Classes," I said with a sigh. "How were your classes? Did you do anything?"

"I drew a picture about me and my summer," she said. "And I played tag at recess."

I miss being in second grade, I thought.

"Did you have a good day?" Grete asked.

"Yeah," I said.

"What did you do?"

"I took a lot of notes."

"With Alexi?"

"In a couple of classes."

"We both had good days, then," she said, skipping the rest of the way home.

I unlocked and opened our front door. Grete and I took off our shoes and placed them in the entry way closet.

"Can I have graham crackers for snack?"

"Mmm—sure," I said. We were only supposed to have fruit or vegetables for a snack, but it was the first day of school and it had been a good day. It was worth taking a chance.

Then I looked in the kitchen. The magic hats were on the table.

So much for a good day. Now anything could happen.

CHAPTER TWO

Mom and Dad met at a university play. It was a student production, and neither of them remembers what the name of the play was. But it had a magic hat in it, a silk black top hat.

As Dad tells the story, he went back to the theater after the play was over and "liberated" the hat. Six months later, he took Mom out for a picnic, and he pulled out the hat to show her some "magic." Then he reached in the magic hat and pulled out a diamond ring. Mom's only slightly less sappy when she tells it. She simply says he stole the hat and then stole her heart.

They got married, obviously. From what I've heard, the first few years were really good. And then Mom's younger sister died.

Mom was a lot older than Aunt Lizzie, who I don't remember. According to Mom, Grandma and Grandpa apparently were too tired to really parent their late "surprise," and they let Lizzie do whatever she wanted. Even though she barely passed enough classes to graduate, my grandparents bought her a brand new Mustang. Two weeks after graduation, she killed herself and four others. They were coming home from a party when she missed a turn and flattened the Mustang against a canyon wall. Blood results showed her alcohol level was nearly three times the legal limit. She probably would have died from alcohol poisoning anyway. I was three when it happened, and even though I don't remember Lizzie, I do remember Mom's wailing sobs when her parents called.

Mom made no secret about how she felt. She blamed her parents for Lizzie's death. She told them, repeatedly and in no uncertain terms, that they had killed Lizzie by not disciplining her. Then Mom developed a whole parenting philosophy program and wrote a book about it.

Maybe you've heard of it: *To No Me Is To Love Me*. She runs seminars for parents of toddlers and preschoolers about how to say no to their children. Seriously. She tells parents how to say no to their kids.

Grandma and Grandpa were gone long before Mom's book came out. Grandma got sick and died less than six months after Lizzie. Grandpa bailed and left the country; no one's heard from him since. I don't think Mom has ever tried to find him.

Mom believes that the problem with society is that too many parents want to be their kids' friends and give them everything they never had when they were growing up. So she's going to change the direction society is going, one toddler's family at a time. I'm pretty sure that she'll have kids hunting her down later in life, looking for revenge, but by then I'll be out of the house.

Dad is a bit more of a free spirit. He is an artist at heart; a fantastic impressionistic painter. But that's not a career that can support a family, so by day he's a graphic artist for an advertising firm. Whenever he feels he's burning out on the job, he'll take a few days off and hide in the basement, painting, making a mess, and having a great time.

When I was six, things started to fall apart for Mom and Dad. I remember Mom storming out twice, staying away for a couple of days before coming home. Finally they found their way to a counselor, and the counselor suggested the magic hat.

Actually, the counselor just suggested a hat: a place to put one hundred different things they wanted to do. The hundred things had to be a mix of things that Dad wanted to do, that Mom wanted to do, and that they both wanted to do. Once a month, according to the counselor, they were to draw an activity from the hat and then do it. The idea was to increase the spontaneity in their relationship and make time for each other.

If that were all it was, the idea probably would have died right there. But Dad came home from the counselor, got out paper, a pen, and the famous magic hat. So he and Mom sat down, and came up with their list. It had things like going to a museum, taking a picnic to the park, going bungee jumping, making dinner together, buying something new for the house, and even just spending two hours together without interruption—no phone, TV, computer or kids.

Over the years, Mom and Dad refined the rules: they have twenty-four hours to at least start the activity, if they want to draw more often than once a month they can, and every six months they add new or favorite activities.

Dad says that the magic hat introduced them, got them married, and saved their marriage. I'm also pretty sure it gave them Grete, because she came along about a year after they started using the magic hat.

And then, last Valentine's Day, Grete and I got our own "magic hats." Grete's was a small Sombrero; mine was an old black fedora. Dad said they were to encourage us to "follow our hearts." At first we were allowed to write our own papers, but the second time we drew from the hats, Grete's slip was, "Adopt six kittens."

So Mom and Dad reviewed the contents of our hats. Dad added more adventurous ones to my slips that read, 'buy a CD,' 'go to a movie,' 'go for a walk,' 'practice 45 bump-set combos,' 'spend the night at Alexi's,' and 'call Raquel.' Mom added more conservative activities to Grete's hat. And they added one more rule to the magic hats: everyone in the family had to support each other's activity, either by helping or just offering encouragement.

Now the magic hats were on the kitchen table. It had been a month since we drew from them, so I shouldn't have been surprised. But I didn't think we'd be drawing on the first day of school, either.

"Magic hats!" Grete said, dancing around, "I love magic hats!" Nothing could stop her enthusiasm. Even though 'adopt six kittens' and 'buy a horse' and 'go on a cruise' weren't in her hat anymore, the excitement of doing whatever the hat said was always a happy surprise for her.

I always felt too anxious about the draw to get excited about it.

Grete looked up at me from under her thick golden eyelashes. "Can we have cookies instead of graham crackers?"

She could read me so easily. She knew how and when to push, and she knew I was afraid of the hat.

"Sure," I said, feeling rebellious. But we couldn't find any cookies, so we were stuck with the graham crackers. "I'll make some frosting." The first day deserved something big.

I had just finished cleaning up when Dad came home. His hours were pretty flexible. Mom's hours, the ones she controlled because she was her own boss, were pretty set.

"Sorry I'm late," he said, kissing me on the cheek. When he saw my puzzled face, he added, "I meant to pick you and Grete up afterschool and take you out for ice cream."

Grete, of course, came back into the kitchen just in time to hear the end of that. "Ice cream!" she shrieked. "Let's go get some!"

"We just had snack," I said.

"Maybe today you can have two snacks. Did you have carrot sticks?" Dad asked.

"We had graham crackers," I said.

"With frosting!" Grete added proudly. So much for keeping that low-key.

Dad glanced at me, a small smile tugging at the corners of his lips. "Next time, I guess."

"But I want ice cream!"

"Next time," Dad said, just a little more firmly. That's all it took. Grete zoomed back to her room, and seconds later we could hear music from her favorite movie.

"She loves that sound track," Dad said.

"I'm so sick of it I could scream."

"I could say the same thing about a few of your CDs too," he said, pulling a dish of fruit salad out of the fridge.

"And yours," I retorted.

"And any music that you hear over and over and over again," he said agreeably. "How was first day of freshman year?"

"Fine."

He cocked an eyebrow at me.

"We might go to New York this year for choir," I said, "And sing when they light the tree at Rocker Square."

"Rockefeller," Dad corrected.

"Whatever."

"When's back to school night?"

"I don't know."

"Is it this week? Next week?"

"Dad..."

"Okay, okay. I'm sure your mother knows."

"Yeah," I said, picking up my pack.

"Any homework tonight?"

"Just some math. I'll have it done before dinner."

"Good."

I went back to my room and shut the door. Grete had gotten the CD player for her birthday last month, and the only time it wasn't on was when she was sleeping. I liked to hear my own music in my room.

I should have done my math, but I wasn't ready to face schoolwork and expectations. So I opened the planner we were given today in homeroom. Everyone in the school had gotten one, and we were supposed to use it for assignments, which I knew Mom would want to go through and check, like I was nine years old instead of in ninth grade. Right now I wanted to go through and mark all the truly important dates—my friends' birthdays and days off from school.

I pulled out my notebook, and copied the dates of my first math and social studies tests down, too. At the back of the book, I found a page for phone numbers. I pulled out my cell phone and wrote everyone's numbers. That reminded me about the new numbers I had gotten today. I put Bridget and Daisy's phone numbers in my cell before I wrote them down. Then I pulled out Dominic's number.

His handwriting was a lot neater than I expected it to be. I wrote his name and number in the planner, and hesitated before putting it in my cell phone, too. It felt daring to have his name and number in my phone.

I logged on Facebook, and checked everyone's status — Mariel was babysitting her cousins, Raquel had swim team practice, Emma had a new crush (everyone had responded to that post, asking who it was, but she wasn't answering yet), and Alexi had posted a new photo of all of us at Mariel's sleepover last weekend.

"Silke is dreading the dangers of the magic hat," I posted. All of my friends knew about the magic hat, and I knew I would get a lot of sympathetic posts in response.

I sent invitations to Bridget and Daisy to become Facebook friends, and then, just out of curiosity, I did a search for Dominic Martin.

Of course, a name like Dominic Martin turned up about three hundred people (unlike Silke Reichard, which I owned all by myself), and even narrowing the search down to our suburb of Chicago still had a forty-four. I skimmed through the profile pics, but didn't see his multi-colored head.

"Girls! Dinner!"

I turned off my computer and headed to the kitchen to wash my hands and set the table.

I didn't have time to wonder about the rampaging rainbow. The magic hats were waiting.

*   *   *

Grete and I had just finished setting the table when Mom came in. Unless there was an accident on the highway, Mom was home within the same ten-minute window every day.

She smiled and said a general "Hello," as she breezed through the kitchen straight back to her room. When she came back two minutes later, wearing faded jeans and a t-shirt, Dad was putting the last plate of steaming rice and fish on the table.

"Mmm, smells good," she said, stopping and kissing him quickly on the cheek.

"Welcome home," he said.

She turned to the table, and I saw her hesitate ever so slightly as she saw the three-hat centerpiece. "Heinrich," she said, turning back to him. "Shouldn't we wait till this weekend?"

"It's been a month," Dad said firmly. He was so laid back and fun about everything else, it was almost scary how closely he monitored the magic hat schedule.

Mom sighed and shook her head, but she was smiling. "So, how was your day, Silke?" she asked as she sat in her chair. "What do you think of high school?"

"It's big," I said.

"Anything exciting?"

"Choir is going to Rockefeller Square for a Christmas concert."

"Who pays for that?" Mom asked.

I shrugged. "We do. The first fundraiser starts next week."

"Who goes with you?"

"I don't know. Ms. Fedderson said she'll talk to parents on back to school night."

"How long will you be gone?"

"I don't know."

"Where will you be staying?"

"I don't know," I repeated. "Ms. Fedderson will tell you about it."

"Okay. We'll talk about it after we know more. How was your day, Grete?"

Grete rehashed her adventures, and then Dad talked about his newest project, and I barely heard them. Mom hadn't ruled out the trip to New York. She said we'd talk about it! There was still a chance—however slight—that she might let me go. I couldn't wait to tell Alexi that she was wrong.

Grete cleared the table and I did the dishes while Mom and

Dad talked a bit more at the table.

"Ready?" Dad asked me when I closed the dishwasher and turned it on.

"Ready," I said, tying to put some enthusiasm into my voice.

"I wanna go first!" Grete crowed.

Mom and Dad looked at me and I shrugged. "Sure."

Eagerly Grete reached into her hat and grabbed a piece of paper, except that it turned out to be two pieces.

"Put one back, Grete," Dad said.

"Can't I see what they are first?"

"Grete," Mom warned, "No cheating."

Grete sighed and put a slip in each hand. Then she did eenie-meenie on her two fists, raising each one in turn. "And—you—are—not—it!" Her left hand was the last one in the air, so she dropped that slip back into the hat and opened the paper in her right.

She shrieked. "Yes, yes, yes!"

"What?" Mom and I asked together.

"I get to paint my room!"

Grete's room still had the Noah's Ark paintings Dad had done to turn the guest room into a nursery, and she had wanted to get rid of the baby stuff for at least a year now.

"You can paint it, but it's only going to be one color, okay?" Mom said. "We'll talk about what color you want tonight, and Silke can take you to buy the paint after school tomorrow."

This was another reason why the magic hat wasn't my favorite family quirk. Even though we were all supposed to be involved and supportive of each other's draws, most of the time I was the one who ended up involved in whatever Grete's draw was. Last month she had pulled "Go to a movie," and I ended up taking her to some stupid animated bird movie on a Friday night instead of hanging out at Mariel's.

"We're just going to buy paint tomorrow, right?" I asked. "I don't have to help her actually paint, do I?"

"I'll paint her room on Wednesday," Dad said. "I was going to take a day off to paint this week anyway."

"Oooh, Daddy, will you make my room to look like one of your paintings?" Grete asked.

Mom laughed. "I don't think so."

"We'll see," Dad said. Mom shot him a look, and I knew that they'd be having another discussion behind their closed bedroom door later tonight.

"Silke?"

I took a deep breath and reached in the fedora, fishing all the way down to the bottom of the hat, trying to feel for a friendly slip of paper.

"Pick a night and a restaurant for dinner this week," I read. "No budget." I looked at Dad. "No way! Really?"

"If the magic hat says so," he said with a smile. "Our turn," he said, nudging the top hat toward Mom.

She looked him in the eye while she reached in for a slip of paper, then she handed it to him.

"Go bowling," he read.

Mom laughed. "We haven't done that in years!"

"Want to go tonight or tomorrow?"

"Mmm—" she glanced at the clock. "Call and see which night has open bowling," she said, "Grete and I will go talk about her room."

Practically dancing, Grete led Mom down the hall while Dad went for the phone book. I stayed at the table, folding, twirling, and tapping the slip of paper.

"Know where you want to go?" he asked as he opened the phone book

I shook my head. We so rarely went out to dinner as a family—only for birthdays and maybe two other times a year—that the pressure of the choice threatened to overwhelm me. And not only did I get to choose where we were going, but I wasn't going to have to do dishes that night, either. It was like a double magic wish.

"If you need any help, let me know."

"We have to go tomorrow night?" I asked.

"We should, but I suppose if you make the reservations

tonight for another night this week, that would be okay too. Why? Where do you want to go that's not open tomorrow?"

I shrugged.

He called a couple of bowling alleys, and started to put the phonebook away. "Can I see it, please?"

"Sure." He handed it to me and headed down the hall after Mom and Grete.

The three of them trooped back to the kitchen just as I was hanging up the phone.

"Got reservations?" Dad asked, rubbing his hands together.

"Yep."

"Where?"

I smiled. "Friday night at six."

Grete frowned. "Daddy asked where, not when."

"Silke knows what she's doing," Dad said to Grete.

"What's she doing?"

"Keeping it a surprise," Mom said dryly. She wasn't amused. Dad gave me a wink.

"Did you pick a color?" I asked Grete, but I was watching Mom. I knew she didn't want Grete going too crazy with her room, and I was trying to see how stressed she was getting.

"Yes!" Grete said, jumping up and down for emphasis. "Blue! Or green!" A slightly pained look crossed Mom's face.

"You'll have to help her look at some samples tomorrow," Dad said, grabbing his car keys from the hook on the wall. "She wants blue or green, but a very pale shade."

"Very, very pale," Mom said.

"Kind of like the way you look right now?" I asked.

She shot me a look. I knew it was practically killing her to imagine Grete's room in blue or green. "We're going bowling tonight," she said instead of responding to my comment. "We shouldn't be out too late. Make sure Grete's in bed on time."

"Can't I come?" Grete asked.

"Not on a school night," Dad replied, swooping in and kissing her on the cheek. "Be good for Silke. And Silke, listen to what your sister says," he added sternly.

Grete giggled.

Mom gave Grete a kiss on the cheek, too, and said, "Be in bed on time."

"I will."

"Make sure you've got all your homework done," Mom said to me. "Back to school night is next Thursday, and I'll be checking to see if you're missing any assignments."

"I know."

"See you in a little while. Make sure everything's locked up."

"I will."

"Don't answer the door."

"Mom!"

"Come on, Teresa, let's act like she's done this before a few hundred times," Dad said.

"I just want to be sure—"

"Silke knows what to do, and she knows our numbers. Let's go."

They left, and I went around and made sure all the doors and windows were locked. I got Grete into bed exactly at eight o'clock, and I was curled up in bed, reading, when they got home, just like I was supposed to be.

They were giggling like a couple of kids as they passed by my bedroom door. I heard them pause, and though I could tell Mom said something and Dad answered, their voices were too indistinct to know what was said. They continued on to their room without checking on me, and when I went to brush my teeth a little while later, their bedroom door was closed and the lights were off.

They must have had a good night.

CHAPTER THREE

Bridget and Daisy were in the same seats when I got to Western Civ the next day, so I slid in behind them again. We started comparing class schedules.

As soon as I said I was in choir, Daisy announced she was going to try out for the school musical next week, and she started trying to get me to go with her. I looked to Bridget for some help, but she just laughed.

"She's been on my case too, but I don't sing. I play volleyball and soccer."

"Me too!" I said. "Well, volleyball. No soccer for me."

I had played on a soccer team when I was five, but one day at practice I got mad at a boy who wouldn't pass me the ball and punched him. Mom pulled me off the team that day, grounded me for a week, and hadn't let me play since. I sometimes wondered if I should ask again, now that a decade had passed and all, but it seemed easier to stay with the sports I had been able to behave in—volleyball and swimming.

The bell rang, and the three of us immediately got out our notebooks. Two guys across the room—the cute ones who had been shoving each other yesterday—weren't so quick, and Mr. Norton ripped into them right away.

"I thought I had been clear yesterday that I expect you to be responsible young adults in this class. That means you will be in your seats, ready to begin class, as soon as the bell rings. If that is too difficult for you to manage, I'll write you a pass to the counselor's office and you may find another class."

"Yes sir," one of them said right away.

The other one muttered something.

"What did you say?" Mr. Norton shouted. And I do mean shouted. On the football field, I'm sure that players thirty or forty yards away would have been able to hear him just fine. In the small, enclosed classroom, it hurt my ears.

The guy just stared back at Mr. Norton. I had a grudging respect for him. Some people seem immune to fear. I often wished I was one of them.

"Go!" Mr. Norton shouted, flinging his arm toward the door. "Just get out!"

The guy stood up and got out, but he wasn't scrambling like I would have been.

"What about you?" Mr. Norton barked at the other guy. "Are you going to shape up or get out?"

"I'll stay," he muttered.

"So you're going to shape up?"

"Yes, sir."

Just as Mr. Norton turned his attention back to the class, a piece of paper landed on my desk.

I froze. Alexi had passed me a note in sixth grade, and the teacher caught us. We both got recess detention for a week. I decided not to tell Mom, but she heard about it a couple of weeks later. Because I had not only broken a school rule but also committed a 'lie of omission' by not telling her, I had been grounded for a month. It happened to be my birthday month too, and she refused to let me have a birthday party, even after the month was over.

My lesson was learned. I hadn't passed a note since.

Mr. Norton hadn't noticed the paper. He turned on the smart board, and a rough outline covering the Euphrates River Valley appeared. I quickly copied down the outline, leaving plenty of lines between each point for further notes, and then carefully opened the note while waiting for the rest of the class to catch up.

> Silke—
> Do u no those guys? Did they go 2 your
> middle school?

I refolded the paper and slipped it under my notebook. Mr.

Norton began the lecture, and I began taking notes. A few moments later, Bridget looked over her shoulder at me and raised her eyebrows. I shrugged and shook my head slightly.

The attendance sheet was making its way around the room, and when Bridget handed it back to me, it had another note with it.

What about hair freak? Do u no him?

I signed my name to the attendance sheet, and then turned around only to discover that Dominic wasn't behind me. Today I was the last person in the last row on my side of the room. I picked up the sheet and took it across to the guy who had decided to stay in class instead of leaving with his friend.

He smiled at me as he took it from my hand, so of course I stumbled over my own feet as I turned to walk back to my desk.

I quickly caught up on the notes, and then I wrote back to Bridget.

Haven't seen any of them b4. The one who's still here is cute!

It took five minutes before Mr. Norton turned around enough for me to risk handing the note up to Bridget.

Five seconds later, the note was back on my desk. A few minutes later, I opened it.

Cute? Try gorgeous!

I grinned and glanced over to the guy. He was staring in my direction. I choked and turned back to face Mr. Norton and his smart board.

When class finally ended, I gathered my notebooks, but as I stood up, I wasn't watching the cute guy across the room. I found myself staring at the empty chair behind me, wondering where Dominic was.

"Grete, it's purple."

"So?"

She had a square of soft lilac, darker than any of the five I had offered her, but much lighter than any of the ones she had spent the last twenty minutes begging for. And really, was a light purple any worse than a pale green or blue?

"Please? Pretty please?" She begged.

I sighed and looked at the sales guy. I could almost hear him thinking pretty please too, just so he could get rid of us.

"We can bring it back, right?" I asked him.

He shook his head. "If we mix you a custom color, it's not exchangeable."

I looked at Grete. After five minutes of arguing with her, I had tried to call Mom and Dad, but it was my bad luck that they were both in meetings. What should I do? Not buy the paint and get in trouble for not doing my job or buy the paint and get in trouble for buying the wrong color?

"Pleeeeease?"

I looked at the sales guy again.

He tapped a square one shade lighter than the one she had asked for and raised his eyebrows. I sighed.

"Okay."

Grete squealed and began dancing around, which made the sales guy smile as he retrieved paint cans and began mixing colors.

"My dad said I should pay for it now and leave it here for him to pick up on the way home," I said.

"Sure," the guy said, "I'll write you a receipt and you can take it up to the register."

"No!" Grete howled. "I want to take the paint home now!"

"We can't," I said. "It's too heavy." Grete opened her mouth and I cut her off. "Don't," I warned. "Don't say anything, or I'll tell him we don't want the paint at all."

Which might not be a bad thing. Right now my only hope was that Dad would see the paint first and either decide to fix it by mixing more white in, or agree it was a good color and stand up to Mom. Somehow, in my gut, I just knew she'd hate it.

Grete snapped her mouth shut, and was pretty good while we waited in line and then paid with Dad's debit card. I was shocked at how expensive the paint was, but I had gotten three five-gallon cans of indoor matte finish just like Dad had asked for, so I shrugged it off. When we got on the city bus, she started again.

"How am I supposed to start painting if I don't have the paint?"

"You're not. Dad will paint your room tomorrow."

"*I* want to paint my room! It's *my* magic slip!"

"Talk to Dad about it," I said with a sigh.

"Where are we going to dinner?" she asked. She bounced around so much in her thoughts it gave me a headache just trying to keep up with her.

"You'll have to wait and see."

"What if I don't want to go?"

"Oh, you'll want to go."

"How do you know?"

"I'm super smart."

Grete rolled her eyes at me like she so often did. "Just tell me."

"Nope," I said. "It's *my* magic slip."

Grete crossed her arms over her chest, stuck her lower lip out, and stared pointedly away from me.

I turned and looked out the window, watching the people and buildings as we zoomed past them.

My magic slip. I wished it really was magic. I wished it could change my life.

*　　　　　　*　　　　　　*

"You have to take them back," Mom said flatly.

"We can't," Grete said with an undeniable tone of victory.

Mom glared at her. "Go to your room!"

"But—"

"Now!"

Tears brimming in her eyes, Grete fled. I would have happily followed, but it merely would have put off the inevitable.

"How could you buy these?" she demanded as I stood alone in front of her.

It was one of the very few days that Dad was running late. When he said he would call and ask Mom to pick up the paint, I immediately started working on a dinner of pork chops, stuffing, steamed carrots and even a batch of blueberry muffins to start making up for my error. But dinner was still in the oven, and I wasn't sure it was enough, anyway.

"She wanted a green or blue room—"

"You got purple!"

"It's almost blue...." I hedged.

"We said a light color!"

"It was on her magic slip—"

"We trusted you to use good judgment! Clearly you don't have any! If I can't trust you to shop for the things we ask you to, I see no reason to allow you to shop at all. Don't make any plans to go to the mall for the next month."

And just like that, going to the mall with my friends on Saturday was gone. I knew better than to argue, so I just nodded.

"And I think you can pay for that paint out of your account as well."

My head snapped up. The paint cost more than I currently had saved up. "No way!" I said. "That's not fair!"

"Life isn't fair," she stated.

"You can't punish me for doing what you asked—I went and bought a light shade of paint for Grete's room because you asked me to!"

"Purple!" Mom growled. "I told her no purple!"

"Well you didn't tell me!" I burst out.

"Watch your tone, young lady!"

The tears were coming, and I hated them, hated my weakness. Why couldn't I ever stand up to her? Stand up for myself?

"I hate this!" I yelled, and I ran from the kitchen, slamming my bedroom door behind me even though I knew it would just provoke her more. I couldn't stop myself. I threw myself on my bed, and counted.

Five seconds later, my door burst open.

"Don't you ever, *ever* yell at me and walk away!"

I rolled to the other side of my bed and stood up, keeping it between us. "I hate this!"

"Hate what?" she demanded with her hands on her hips. "Hate me?"

I had to answer carefully here. It would be so easy to say yes—I did hate her rules and her temper and her constant demands—but she was my mother, and I didn't hate *her*. I just hated everything she believed.

"I hate the way you do everything!" I tried to keep my voice steady, but it broke on the last word.

"You hate the way I keep you safe and teach you to be a successful, productive person and show you how you can be better? You hate the way I work hard every day to make sure that you have everything you need?"

"What's going on?" Dad asked from behind her.

"Your daughter was unable to make a simple purchase for us and when I corrected her decision, she decided that she hates me."

"Unbelievable!" I shouted, making her flinch. "You are so incredibly, stupidly unbelievable!"

"Did you just call me stupid?"

"Teresa," Dad said softly, "why don't you go wait in the kitchen?"

"But—"

"You both need time to calm down," he said, still using his

soothing tone. "You wait in the kitchen, Silke can wait here, and we'll have a calm discussion in a little while and get this all sorted out."

"There's nothing to sort out!" Mom was talking to Dad but staring me down. "She's being defiant and disrespectful, and I will not stand for it."

"Teresa," Dad said sharply before I could retort.

She turned her head and stared at Dad for a long second. Finally she spun around and stalked out of my room.

"Dad—"

He held up his hand. "You and Mom both need to calm down. I won't talk to either of you until I talk to both of you together. I won't be put in the middle." He stepped out of my room, pulling my door shut behind him.

I flopped back down on my bed, taking deep breaths and trying to organize my thoughts. Having Dad at the table with Mom and me would help, but only because he wouldn't let her run over me. I'd still have to explain what I had said and what I meant. I'd have to explain how I felt. Somehow, no matter what I said, she always managed to make how I felt sound wrong.

Sooner than I was ready, there was a knock and then my door popped open. Dad stuck his head in. "Time to come to the kitchen."

He was gone before I could ask for more time. I took a deep breath and then another one. I didn't want to have a show down. I hated being in trouble. I always felt like I was in trouble, even though I had never done anything bad. Ever.

I stepped into the hall and had taken two steps towards the kitchen when I heard Grete behind me. "Silke?" she said softly.

I looked behind me. She was standing in her bedroom doorway, wide-eyed and pale. "I'm sorry," she whispered, tears spilling over and running down her cheeks.

I gave her a quick hug and tried to smile, and then I headed toward the kitchen.

Dad was sitting next to Mom, so if I sat next to Dad, I'd be looking directly at Mom, or if I wanted to look directly at Dad, then I had to sit next to Mom. I sat next to Dad. Mom was staring at me, but I couldn't look at her. Instead, I turned my head to watch Dad.

The seconds dripped by slowly, like a pinprick hole being used to empty a gallon jug. I wasn't going to speak first. I didn't have a list of grievances; I was defending myself against inaccurate accusations. And I knew that Dad wasn't going to start; he was here to keep us on track, not to get involved or mediate. So, as usual, we were waiting for Mom to set the pace.

She seemed to be having a hard time finding her words, which was very unusual.

Since it was supposed to be a discussion between Mom and me, I was surprised when Dad began, "Painting a room purple will not make Grete be like Lizzie."

"That is *not* what this is about," Mom snapped.

"You didn't tell me you didn't like purple," I muttered, feeling bad that this was bringing back memories of her sister.

"Then what is it about?" Dad asked Mom, still using a mild tone.

"I will not have a defiant, disruptive teenager in my house. That is not an option."

"I am a straight-A student, a responsible big sister, a hard-working daughter, and the farthest thing from a defiant, disruptive teenager," I said, still staring at Dad instead of looking at Mom. I knew if I did, I'd break into tears again. "I am insulted that you would label me like that."

"When you shout at me, you're being defiant," Mom snapped.

"When you raise your voice to me, you're escalating the anger," I retorted, using the terms she preached at her seminars all the time. I fought hard not to match her increased volume.

Dad's lips twitched, whether because he was stopping himself from saying something or stopping a smile, I couldn't tell.

I heard Mom's loud exhale, and knew she was blowing her breath up through her bangs because it was my point, but I wasn't going to look at her.

"You didn't complete your job today."

"I did—"

"You allowed your seven-year-old sister to make a decision for you."

"I followed the instructions I was given and reached the best possible compromise I could."

"You should have just said no!" Mom thumped her hand on the table. "Just because a child wants something doesn't mean you give in. Children need boundaries!"

"She had boundaries—blue or green and a light color. It's a light purple, which is technically a shade of blue, and when you look at the scale of purples, it's very light. You didn't tell me no purple. If you don't set clear guidelines, you're setting your child up for failure, which is, in reality, your failure and not theirs," I added.

Once again Dad's lips twitched, but this time it was clearly because he was trying not to smile. I was practically reciting Mom's lecture back to her to defend myself.

"You must be able to say no to Grete."

"She's not my child. Maybe I need to be able to say no to my parents when they set me up for failure."

Dad frowned.

"We didn't set you up—" Mom began.

"You asked me to do something that you wanted to control, not me."

"There you go, being defiant again!"

"Let's clarify," I said, once again using her terms, "You consider it defiance when I'm pointing out the impossible position you put me in?"

"Heinrich, I can't do this!" she exclaimed. "She's being difficult."

"I'm being calm and logical," I countered.

"Heinrich!"

Dad sighed. "Do you really want me to say something?"

"Yes!"

"I talked to Grete," he said, "And she told me that Silke tried to talk her into different colors, but that Grete didn't want them. She forgot that you said no purple. Grete wanted to paint her room, like the magic hat said she could. She's awfully upset."

"Heinrich—"

"Grete was crying because she got Silke in trouble, not because you took her CD player from her."

"Silke wouldn't be in trouble if she had just said no—"

"That's not true," I interrupted. "If I had said no and come home without purchasing the paint, I would have been in trouble for not doing my job. No matter what I did today, I was going to be in trouble." The tears were coming again. I was tired of fighting them. "I work so hard and I'm never in trouble with anyone else. But I'm always in trouble with *you*!"

"That's not true—"

"How is it I can't do anything right? If I get a B, you want an A. If I get an A, it should be an A plus. I'm never good enough for you!" I could barely get the last words out. Blindly, I pushed away from the table and ran back to my room.

I managed to shut my door instead of slamming it, but I fell on my bed, sobbing.

It was all so stupid, and yet I couldn't help feeling my entire world was awful. Maybe my parents weren't divorced or on drugs or poor, but they still managed to make my life hell. Defiant and disruptive? Me? I couldn't even look someone in the eye when they were mad at me.

I heard the bedroom door open but I didn't lift my head from the pillows. Someone sat on the edge of my bed, but they didn't touch me or say anything for a long time. Finally I got my breathing back under control, and my tears stopped. I wanted to move my face away from the wet pillow, but I didn't want to look up. I sniffled and closed my eyes.

"I'm sorry," Mom's voice sounded stilted. "I'm sorry that you think I'm so awful. I'm trying to do my best for you. I know you work hard, but I'd think you realize that Dad and I work hard, too. And that paint was very expensive. I gave you a cell phone; if you were unsure about the color, you could have at least called."

"I did!" I shouted into the pillow, which made me feel better and muffled my voice enough that she couldn't get mad at me. "I called both of you! You were in meetings!"

"You didn't tell me that," Mom said, as if it was my fault.

"You didn't give me the chance."

She sighed. "I'm sorry," she repeated. "Perhaps I over reacted a bit."

With my face safely hidden in the pillow, I rolled my eyes. *A bit?*

"Dad thinks he can work with the color anyway. So…" she hesitated, and I was intrigued enough to lift my head and look at her. "You're not grounded from the mall."

I closed my mouth against the "Yes!" I wanted to holler. I shouldn't celebrate over that—it was merely righting the wrong; it wasn't a reward of any kind.

She reached out and put her hand on my head, smoothing my hair down. "I really am sorry, Silke," she said. "You know I love you."

I nodded.

She stood up. "Let's go have dinner."

I had forgotten about the pork chops.

"Be right there."

She left, and I heard her go to Grete's room. I went to the bathroom to splash cold water on my face. My eyes were bloodshot and puffy and my throat hurt. I didn't want to eat, but I didn't want to jump from one scene to another. It was a Reichard family rule that we all ate dinner together.

Mom and I didn't talk much during dinner, but Grete made up for it. Even being grounded from her music couldn't dampen her excitement about painting her room. She was super thrilled that Dad had promised she'd be able to help with some of work after school tomorrow.

"Can I paint some flowers?"

"No!" Mom said at the same time Dad said, "Sure."

"Heinrich, she's too young—"

"To express her artistic side? Nonsense." Then he added, "I'll help her."

Mom stabbed her pork chop.

"I'm sure looking forward to going out to dinner on Friday, aren't you?" Dad asked the table at large.

"No," Grete said instantly.

"Why not?"

"Silke won't tell me where we're going."

"I think she'll have to when we get in the car."

Grete glared at me. "I bet she just gives us directions."

"Exactly," I said. I hadn't thought about it before, but I'd just get directions from the computer.

"Let's hope your plans cause less trouble than Grete's," Mom muttered.

Although I agreed with her, I was gratified when Dad said, "Nothing from the magic hat causes trouble. It's good to try new things."

CHAPTER FOUR

Bridget and Daisy joined our group for lunch on Wednesday. As usual, boys ended up being the main topic of conversation.

Emma was happy because her math teacher had been forced to adjust the seating chart in class, and Adrian Simmonds was now sitting next to her. Alexi immediately pointed out that in the art rooms, there were tables instead of desks, so Adrian was really sitting *next* to her in class, whereas he was only sitting *near* Emma.

"I found out the guy's name," Bridget said to me.

"Oh?" I said, while Mariel asked, "What guy?"

"There's a super-hot guy in our social studies class," Bridget said. "Danny McCauley."

"Danny McCauley," I repeated slowly, seeing how it sounded.

"Is he the freaky dude?" Alexi asked me. "The amok rainbow?"

"No, that's Dominic."

"Right," she said, nodding, while Bridget choked on her drink.

"Amok rainbow?" she asked. "Who talks like that?"

"Silke does," Alexi said calmly. "She reads a lot and helps us increase our vocabulary. This week's word is 'amok'."

"Thanks," I said, rolling my eyes. It was embarrassing that she actually bragged about what a nerd I was.

"I think Dominic's pretty cute, too," Bridget said, "In a freaky, amok-ey kind of way."

"Gross!" Daisy cried. "He is so not cute in any kind of way."

"Sure he is," Bridget dug in. "He's got gorgeous eyes."

"Eyes do not make a guy cute," Daisy declared, and the debate was on.

I picked at my food and let them argue. I had already scanned the cafeteria, and I knew that Dominic wasn't here. I hadn't seen him in the halls, either. I had only seen him that first day of class, but for some reason, I kept thinking about him. There was something about him that I found fascinating, though I couldn't say exactly what it was. It bothered me to discover that Bridget had been thinking about him too.

"Silke? You here?"

I looked up to find Mariel staring at me. "Sorry," I made myself grin. "Zoning."

"You coming on Saturday?"

"I want to, but I don't know if I can yet."

"Spend the night at my house," Emma said suddenly. "Then you don't have to ask, we'll just go together."

"But we want to go at lunch time," Mariel objected.

"I know. She can just come over at noon to study English and Spanish, and then we'll go to the mall."

"I don't know," Alexi said to me, "You don't want to get in trouble."

Usually Alexi's concern about my mother helped me stay under control. Now, however, I wanted to show them both. "I'll come study, Emma. We'll go practice our Spanish at the mall by ordering *taquito con queso, muy caliente, por favor*," I grinned, ignoring Alexi as she shook her head.

"What did you say?" Emma asked.

"At least I won't be lying," I laughed, "You do need to study."

*   *   *

Daisy, Bridget, and I walked into Mr. Norton's class together. Danny McCauley was already in his seat, notebook open.

And Dominic was in his seat, too.

His hair was parted at a strange angle, and at first I thought he had re-dyed his hair because it looked orange. As I got closer, though, I realized that the layer of hair currently on top was orange, but the rest of the colors were still peeking out from underneath.

"Want to switch seats?" Bridget whispered to me.

"That's okay," I said, stepping in front of her and sitting in my usual desk.

Almost immediately, Dominic was tapping my shoulder. "Can I see your notes from yesterday?"

I unclipped the pages from my notebook and handed them to him.

"Wow," he said, looking at each side of the paper. "Did you write every single word he said?"

"No. I could read this to you, you know, if you're going have trouble with the big words."

"I was going to offer to tutor you in note taking, actually, because you don't have to write *every* word—just the ones that matter."

I reached for the pages. He held them away and shook his head with a smile.

"Were you sick yesterday?"

"Nah," he said, already scribbling notes on his own paper.

I waited but that seemed to be all he was going to say. "So where were you?"

"Suspended."

The bell rang, and I turned around gratefully. I had no idea what to say to him after that. Who got suspended on the second day of school?

There were ten minutes left in class when Dominic tapped me on my shoulder again. I turned around.

"Is there something you'd like to share with the class?" Mr. Norton barked.

"Uhhh—" I was holding the folded pages Dominic had just slipped into my hand.

"Perhaps you'd like to read that out loud to the class?" Mr. Norton was walking toward me.

"Uhh—" I really could not get my brain to work, let alone

get my mouth to form words.

"That might take a while," Dominic said from behind me. "They're the notes from yesterday. She let me see them since I was absent. There are a lot of details."

By now Mr. Norton was standing in front of my desk. He held out his hand, and I gave him the pages. He unfolded them and stared at them for a long second.

Then he smiled, a real smile, not the scary one he usually used. "Very nice notes indeed, Ms. Reichard." I tried not to gape as he handed the notes back to me. How did he know my name?

Mr. Norton resumed the lecture, and I clipped my notes back in place. The sign in sheet came around, and this time I was ready for Bridget's note. I removed the extra page, signed my name to the list, and handed it back to Dominic. He smiled at me, and my internal organs felt a jolt.

I turned back to my notes and then carefully opened the small page from Bridget.

> *Lucky!*
> *Maybe he is sorta cute in a freakishly*
> *amuck way.*
>
> *u go girl!*

Briefly I thought about correcting Bridget's spelling, but then I decided that was too nerdy even for me. I figured the other handwriting was from Daisy. I quickly put the note in my binder and went back to writing about the Euphrates River Valley. There was no way I was going to risk Mr. Norton asking to see it!

A few minutes later, I pulled a loose sheet from my notebook. I wrote quickly, folded it over twice, and then waited until Mr. Norton was facing the other side of the classroom before I dropped it over Daisy's shoulder. She caught it and almost as soon as she opened it, she whipped around to stare at me, her mouth hanging open.

Fortunately, the bell rang. As we were all gathering our stuff, Mr. Norton raised his voice and said, "I hope all of you have been taking as complete notes as Ms. Reichard; otherwise, tomorrow's quiz may be painful."

We all groaned. Dominic laid his hand on my shoulder and rumbled almost directly into my ear. "Thanks!" And then he was gone, leaving goosebumps running down my neck.

"You cannot be serious!" Daisy was hissing at me, her eyes flickering rapidly between me and Danny McCauley. "Are you sure? Really?"

"What?" Bridget asked.

But Daisy was shaking her head, looking slightly bug-eyed. Danny McCauley was approaching.

"Hi," he said to Daisy with an easy smile. "I think we have study hall together, don't we?"

"Third hour?" Daisy asked, as if during lunch she hadn't been bragging that he sat two seats to the left and three seats in front of her.

"Yeah," he bobbed his head. "Third hour. Listen, my notes from the first day aren't that great. Could I see yours tomorrow in study hall?"

"Sure," Daisy said. "No problem."

"Great. Thanks. See you tomorrow," he said, and he headed out of the classroom.

Daisy waited until he was out of the room, and then she squealed. "Did you hear that?" She exclaimed. "He is sooo cute!"

"I told you he was staring at you all period," I said.

"I know you did," Daisy said, clutching the note to her chest. "I can't believe he was looking at me!"

"Couldn't take his eyes off you," Mr. Norton said dryly.

We all jumped. We had forgotten he was in the room. We sped from the room in a silent pack, but when we reached the hall, Bridget and I nearly collapsed with laughter. Daisy, meanwhile, was brick red and looked to be on the verge of tears.

I put my arm around her shoulders. "You'll be all right," I assured her. "Danny likes you."

Daisy sniffed. "You really think so?"

"He couldn't take his eyes off you," Bridget said in a gruff voice, imitating Mr. Norton, and she and I were laughing again. This time, Daisy joined us.

*   *   *

I walked into the house alone that afternoon. I stopped to pick Grete up, just like always, but she had run home ahead of me, desperately eager to see her new room.

I followed at a slower pace, texting Mariel and Emma about social studies class and our plans for the weekend.

"Come look, come look!" Grete screeched, running up to me before I got in the door. She grabbed my hand and nearly yanked my arm out of the socket. "It's soooo beautiful!!"

I let her drag me down the hall to her room. She let go of my hand at the door and I stopped short. She was right; it was beautiful. Dad had done magic with the paint, starting it dark near the ceiling and fading as it moved down the wall to nearly white where it met the floor. It was a very dreamy effect.

"Look look look!" Grete said, coming back to grab my arm again. "Come see, come see!" She took me across the room, stopping me in front of a two by two white square in the middle of the wall, maybe three feet off the ground. It was bordered by about an inch of brown paint, shaded so that it almost looked three-dimensional, like a frame. She was dancing around.

"What is this?" I asked.

"It's where I get to paint!" She hollered, jumping up as high as she could. "I get to paint flowers, any way I want them!"

I looked at Dad. He looked so happy in his splattered painter jeans and long sleeved t-shirt, and had purple paint flecks in his hair. He was squirting small mounds of paint on to his palette.

"She's going to paint flowers?"

"Inside the frame," he agreed. "She can paint whatever she wants in the frame, but nowhere else," he added, clearly repeating himself to Grete.

"Cool," I said.

"Want to paint your room?" Grete asked me. She had found her smock and was pulling it on over her school clothes. "Daddy and I will help."

"It's not in my magic hat," I said.

"We could fix that," Dad offered.

"No thanks."

"You sure?"

"Yep."

"Okay. Wait, Grete, let me show you what to do, just a second."

I left them to their painting. A Spanish verb worksheet and a periodic table questionnaire only took me twenty minutes to finish, and then I got online.

Bridget and Daisy had both accepted my friend invitations, and Daisy had hit me with a snowball. I returned it, and threw one to everyone else before checking new status updates.

When we all sat down to eat that night, Grete was still gushing about her room. Mom liked it too.

"We could do the same thing in our room," Dad said.

"No thanks," she said quickly.

*   *   *

"What's fondue?" Grete asked Friday night as we all climbed out of the car.

"Expensive," Mom muttered.

"The hat said no budget," I said, looking at Dad for confirmation.

"I'm starting to worry about the bad influence of the hat."

"Teresa," Dad said, "We don't go out often. Relax and enjoy it."

"Look!" Grete squealed as we followed the waitress to our table. "There are pots on the tables!"

"Yes," the waitress said with a smile. "You get to cook your own dinner."

"And yet we get to pay for it," Mom muttered.

"Teresa," Dad said again.

She plastered a smile on her face. Dad crossed his eyes at her. Mom's smile became genuine. He stuck his tongue out and she giggled.

"I'm sorry," she said to all of us. "It's just been a rough week."

"So let's enjoy a great evening," Dad said.

We sat at the table, dipping our way through the meal, laughing and talking, for nearly three hours. It was the best night I could remember in a long, long time.

*   *   *

Saturday morning I was able to satisfy Mom that I had finished all of my homework for the weekend, and she allowed me to go to Emma's for our "study session."

"Help me," I said to Emma as soon as we got to her bedroom. "I need a make over."

"No problem!" she said, "You know I love dressing you up." And she made me over. She pulled some of my hair up in a loose topknot, and then curled the ends, using an almost obscene amount of hair spray to make them stay curled. Then I selected a dark purple eye shadow, and she used a nice pink to highlight it.

"Can I look in your closet?" I asked.

"Nope," she said cheerfully, "You finish putting the eyeliner and mascara on while I pick out what you're going to wear."

I felt almost naked in the tiered white miniskirt and spaghetti strap top that Emma laid out for me. But when I saw myself in the mirror, I loved it. I wished Mom would let me dress like this, instead of making me sneak around.

Emma's mom drove us over to the mall and made us promise to meet her at two o'clock sharp. "Every minute you're late—" she began.

"Is a free hour of babysitting," Emma finished with her, and they laughed. I loved hanging out with Emma's family. They had about half as many rules and twice as much fun as my family did. They didn't need a magic hat to be spontaneous— they just were.

Almost as soon as we walked in the mall door, Emma's phone rang. We agreed to meet Mariel, Alexi, and Daisy in the food court in an hour. Until then, Emma and I wandered around the stores. It took a little while to forget that I was breaking the rules, but by the time we got to the second store, I was relaxed and enjoying myself.

Emma bought a pair of shoes and a sweater. She babysat her two little brothers every other Friday night, so she almost always had cash on hand. I had some birthday money left, but I was saving it for a new pair of jeans, so I only had enough for the food court today.

Mom didn't believe in allowances, and she considered it part of my family obligation to watch Grete on the nights that she and Dad went out. Usually I could ask for a little shopping money when I went out, but I didn't want to ask today. It would be hard to explain why I needed shopping money when I was supposed to be having a study session at Emma's.

I had fun hanging out with Emma anyway, even without money. It was so much better than being at home.

We went to the food court ten minutes early so we could get a good table, but the others were already there. They had gotten a table in plain view of the Lickin' Chicken, and Adrian Simmonds was behind the counter.

"Silke, you look great!" Daisy said. "You should wear that to school!"

"As long as you call me first," Mariel said, "We almost look like twins!" She was wearing the same skirt in a pale blue with a dark blue strappy shirt.

"Don't worry," I replied, "You know I can't wear this to school."

"It's too bad," Mariel said sympathetically, "'Cause you look great in it!"

We went in shifts to order our food, so we could keep our table and be as visible as possible to all of the guys. Emma and I went to Waco Taco and ordered our *taquitos con queso, por favor*, but Alexi of course ordered from Lickin' Chicken. We made her go to the counter alone, and tried to act casual, but we were totally obvious.

"I can't believe you guys!" Alexi hissed when she came back with her tray. Her face was bright red. "Adrian asked if you all were watching me so carefully because it was my first time at the mall!"

We all laughed, and Daisy and I really laughed when Alexi told Mariel it was her turn to go up to the counter. "I'm glad I went first," she said as Mariel got up, "At least I didn't have to explain why we were going one at a time instead of together."

Mariel came back, smirking, and Alexi was immediately suspicious.

"What happened?"

"It was just like you said."

"Oh?" Alexi asked.

"Adrian asked why we didn't come up to order together." Mariel had her head tilted to one side and was smiling at her chicken sandwich as she unwrapped it.

Alexi's eyes narrowed. "What did you say?"

Mariel had taken a bite before Alexi finished the question, and she took her time chewing carefully and then taking a drink and wiping her mouth with a napkin. "I just told him the truth," and she took another bite.

"Mariel!" Alexi snapped. "*What* did you say?"

Mariel held up a finger and pointed to her mouth while she chewed.

"Oh, just talk with your mouth full! It's not like your mother's here!" I exclaimed.

"No, but yours is," a voice said behind me.

I didn't need to see Alexi's suddenly pale face looking past my shoulder to know that Mom was right behind me, and I didn't need to see Mom's face to know that she was pissed.

"Did you forget to tell me that your study session was meeting at the mall today?"

I was so totally busted. There wasn't any way I could wipe the makeup off my face, let alone put my regular clothes on. I took a deep breath and began cleaning up my half-eaten *taquito*. "I'll see you Monday," I said to everyone as I got up.

"What are you wearing?" Mom demanded as I turned around and she got a look at me. "You look like a....a slut!"

Mariel squeaked and I felt my face flush. "Mom!"

"Home. Now!"

Mom stalked out of the food court, and miserably I followed her.

Just before we reached the mall doors, I heard, "Silke? Damn, girl, you look good!"

I looked up. "Dominic!"

Today his hair was in three ponytails, parted in such a way that they all showed blue. He was wearing what I now recognized as his regular clothes: faded t-shirt under a flannel shirt, torn jeans, and high-top sneakers. And I noticed something new.

"When did you get your lip pierced?" A small hoop ring was on the side of his lower lip.

"Yesterday," he said with a big grin. "Like it?"

"It's—"

"Time to go!" my mother said sharply, yanking my arm.

"Mom! Stop it!"

But she continued to drag me away.

"Mom, you're embarrassing me!"

"In front of that?" she sneered.

I glanced over my shoulder. I thought Dominic would already be slouching away, and I was shocked to see him staring after me. My stomach rolled, not in an unpleasant way.

"You should be embarrassed to be *talking* to him! How does he even know your name?"

"He's in my class."

She was muttering about how parents who don't say no to their children are only hurting themselves and the kids, that it is in fact a disservice to society not to say no to your children, and kept pulling me after her, even though we were in the parking lot and Dominic was far behind. How could I possibly face him on Monday?

She didn't say anything to me the whole drive home, just continued her muttering, moving on to something about the pathetic shape of public education in general and my high school in particular and I knew that she was really angry. I didn't care. I was mad, too.

We walked into the house. I turned to talk to her, but she just pointed down the hallway. "Go clean that gunk off your face and find some decent clothes."

As I walked down the hall to my room, I heard Dad say, "You're back quickly. You got everything that fast?"

"No," there was a thump and I could picture Mom as she slammed her purse on the kitchen table. "You're daughter snuck out to the mall in a completely inappropriate skirt."

"What? I thought she looked fine."

"She was showing entirely too much skin."

"Maybe you need to lighten up a little, Teresa."

"Heinrich, if we lose control now, we'll never get it back. We must be firm with her."

"But—"

"No. She's pushing boundaries, and we must push back."

I shut my door behind me and turned on my radio. It couldn't drown out my thoughts, but it did a good job drowning out the rest of their conversation. Not that there would be much of one. Dad might try, but he wasn't strong enough to stand up to Mom. Just like me. I had a lot of great thoughts, but I never shared them with her.

It bugged the crap out of me that she thought just by hanging out at the mall with my friends I was going to turn into a delinquent. Like having a social life would destroy my GPA. Like wearing a short skirt once in a while would get me pregnant.

I knew better. I wasn't going to be like Lizzie. I didn't have enough of a spine to talk back to my own mother; how could I be a rebel?

My cell phone buzzed, and I grabbed it out of my purse.

U ok? The text from Alexi read.

Who knows? I texted back. I almost added, *Who cares?* Instead, I texted, *U ok?*

Yes. M told A i like him.

No way!

He just ?ed 4 my #

Wtg, I texted back, and flopped down on my bed. At least my best friend was having a good day.

CHAPTER FIVE

The week sped by, even though I was grounded for two weeks for not asking Mom and Dad if I could go to the mall with Emma, and wearing 'inappropriate clothing' while there. Mom took my computer and phone away Saturday night, but she had to give me the phone back on Monday morning. Surprisingly, she also gave me my computer privileges back on Wednesday.

On the way to school, Alexi caught me up on the weekend.

She had been pissed at Mariel at first, but forgave her when Adrian had come out to the table and asked for her phone number. On Sunday they went to the movies. Daisy stayed the night at her house on Saturday, and they found Danny McCauley on Facebook and spent three hours passing cyber gifts back and forth.

"And of course, we all feel awful that you got in trouble," Alexi finished.

Classes were easy and boring, and I didn't have much homework, which actually bugged me because I was confined to my room and needed something to do. I had read through almost all of my books, I was only allowed on the computer if I was doing homework, and I wasn't even allowed to watch my hour of TV. I entertained myself Monday night by getting really creative in the kitchen and making a three-course meal, but when I saw how much Mom enjoyed it, I wished I hadn't.

I read to Grete every afternoon, much to her delight, but as soon as we had finished her required fifteen minutes of reading, she shot off to watch her hour of TV.

I brought the exercise ball into my room and did so many crunches on Tuesday night that I could hardly stand up straight on Wednesday.

I shouldn't have worried about what Dominic would say about my mother's comments, because Dominic wasn't at school.

When he was gone Monday and Tuesday, I simply thought that he was suspended again. By Thursday, though, I was wondering if he was sick. Or had moved. Or dropped out. I found the thought strangely distressing.

*   *   *

"Silke!" Grete hurtled out of her school Thursday afternoon. "I won! I won!"

"What did you win?"

"Melvin!" she exclaimed, grabbing my hand with both of hers and dragging me towards her classroom door.

"Melvin?"

"Our rat!"

"Your what?"

By now she had me inside her classroom.

"Here she is, Ms. DeLoach!" Grete cried.

Grete's teacher smiled. "Good. I'm glad you don't have to walk home alone."

"I'm sorry," I said, "But I don't understand—"

"Each weekend, a different student gets to take Melvin home. Today we drew Grete's name."

"So we'll come get him tomorrow?"

"Actually," Ms. DeLoach said, "I'm going to a conference tomorrow, so I'd like to send Melvin home tonight, to make sure the sub doesn't forget to send him home with someone."

"I don't think my mother will like this."

"Oh, she already said yes," Ms. DeLoach assured me. "At back to school night, I sent a sign up sheet around, and only the children whose parents signed up have their name in the drawing hat. Not everyone wants a rat for the weekend."

"No kidding," I said, staring at the plastic cage Grete was lifting from a bookshelf. Melvin was a white rat, complete with bald pink tail and blood red eyes. Not the kind of pet Mom would want to have in the house. But if Mom had signed the sheet, then we were taking him home.

"Here, Grete," I said, "Let me take him."

"I wanna carry him!"

"You can't carry him all the way home."

"But—"

"Grete," Ms. DeLoach said firmly, "This is why we were waiting for your sister, remember?"

Grete got her stubborn I'm-going-to-argue look on her face, but then she took a deep breath and said, "Okay."

"Could you carry my pack for me?" I asked her. She made a face. "It's pretty light."

"Okay."

So on Thursday I walked into my house carrying a rat and facing another ten days of being grounded. As I set Melvin on Grete's dresser, I figured things couldn't get much worse.

"Magic hats!" Grete shrieked from the kitchen.

Of course, I thought. *I never catch a break.*

*   *   *

"No," Mom said when she walked into the kitchen that evening.

Dad and I both turned from the counter, where we were making an exotic dinner consisting of hotdogs, Hamburger Helper and steamed green beans. "I'm sorry?" Dad said blankly.

"No," she repeated, setting her briefcase down. "I can't. I can't deal with the hats tonight."

Dad was drying his hands on a dishtowel as he walked toward her. "You know the deal," he said softly.

"Not this week," she practically groaned.

"When the hats get put on the table—"

"Heinrich—"

"We've had another rough week," Dad said. "We all need a

little pick me up."

"There's no guarantee that the magic hat will pick me up. It certainly didn't last time."

"Not true. We had a ball bowling—"

"Ha, ha," she said, but she was leaning into his chest.

"Grete is thrilled with her room—"

"I think she'll hate it in less than a year and we'll have to—"

"And Silke took us out for a wonderful dinner—"

"We—" she started, but then she caught sight of me over Dad's shoulder and she stopped. "Yes. It was a wonderful dinner. But the hats should wait till next week, Labor Day weekend is—"

"No."

"But we don't have time right now…."

"This is a reason to make time," Dad reminded her. "Besides, we don't know what we're going to draw. It could be something as simple as going to a movie or making dinner together."

A strange look crossed Mom's face. Dad kissed her and I turned back to the green beans. I could hear them murmuring, and then Mom sighed. "Okay, okay."

Grete came charging into the kitchen, and Mom screeched. It was a sound I had never heard from Mom before. "What is that?"

"It's Melvin," Grete said, skidding to a halt in front of Mom.

Mom backed up so fast she ran into the wall. "It's a rat!"

"Well, yeah," Grete said, sounding confused.

"Why do you have a rat?"

"I get to have him this weekend."

"Says who?"

"Says you." Grete was holding Melvin with both hands, and he suddenly wriggled free and climbed up on her shoulder.

"I certainly do not!"

Dad cleared his throat. Mom looked up at him. "Do you remember Grete's back to school night?" he asked.

"Yes…."

"Do you remember the clipboard of sheets the teacher passed around? For volunteers?"

"Yes...."

"One of the sheets involved agreeing to let our child bring the class pet home on weekends."

Mom stared up at Dad. "Oh, no."

He raised his eyebrows. "Yes."

"I signed up for cupcakes and...and the Valentine party."

"I think maybe you signed the wrong sheet."

Mom leaned her forehead against Dad's chest. And I think she whimpered.

"Grete," Dad said gently, "It's dinner time. Put Melvin back. Wash you hands before you come back." As Grete disappeared down the hall, he added, "I'll call Ms. DeLoach and take Grete's name off the rat list tomorrow."

"She won't be there tomorrow," I said. "That's why Melvin came home today."

"I'll be sure to call on Monday, then," Mom said firmly.

We ate dinner with the regular how-was-your-day kind of conversations, but no one was really bubbling over with enthusiasm, except, of course, Grete.

"I get two magic hats today," she chattered. "But Ms. DeLoach's magic hat is just a shoe box."

"And she doesn't have to do anything," Mom grumbled.

"Teresa," Dad warned.

"Who gets to draw first this time?" Grete asked eagerly.

No one said anything.

"Can I go first *again*?" she whispered.

"Sure," I said.

"Really?" her eyes were wide.

"Really," Dad said. "Here," he held her hat out towards her. "Go ahead."

Grete grinned and she didn't wait for him to ask twice. Her hand dove into the hat and she pulled out a paper pinched between her thumb and forefinger.

She opened the paper and gasped. She started squealing,

raising the volume almost like a teakettle.

"What's it say?" Dad asked, smiling at her enthusiasm.

"It says I can have a sleepover!" She was bouncing in her seat. "A sleepover!"

I couldn't believe it. Grete had been asking to have a sleepover almost as long as she had been asking to paint her room. Mom didn't think she was old enough yet. And now Grete got both of them in less than two weeks.

"Silke?" Mom held my hat out. I reached out slowly.

"Try something new,'" I read out loud. "Try something new? What does that mean?"

"Well," Mom said dryly, "I think it means to try something you haven't done before."

"Like what?"

"Maybe wearing a different style of clothes," Dad suggested, "Or calling someone you've just met."

"Or listening to classical music for a week," Mom said.

"Or going to a high school football game?" I asked.

"Exactly!" Dad beamed. "You get to step out of your comfort zone."

I tried not to grin at him. 'Trying something new' was certainly something he had put in my hat for me, but maybe I could make it work to my advantage.

Dad held the top hat out to Mom. "Your turn," he said sweetly.

"Why thank you," she said. She had a very strange look on her face and she hardly even glanced away from him long enough to look at the piece of paper she was holding before she said, "Go to Las Vegas."

Dad dropped the hat on the table. "No!" He pulled the sheet out of her hand.

"I'm so glad you feel the same—"

"We're going to Vegas, baby!" he crowed. "I've wanted to take you to Vegas for—"

"Heinrich! No! We can't go!"

"What? Why not? Of course we can go!"

"Not *now*. Maybe for Labor Day weekend."

"That's two weeks away," Dad said. "You know the rules. Forty-eight hours, maximum."

"No."

"The hat says—"

"But we just drew a few days ago! I didn't expect—at least give us more time to do this one—it's so big! We could make the reservations now and go for Labor Day—"

"Teresa—"

"NO! The hat doesn't rule us!" She slammed her hand down on the table. "No! No!" She pushed back from the table and strode from the room.

Standing up, Dad gave me an apologetic look. He patted the top of Grete's head as he went out after Mom.

Grete cleared the table while I did the dishes. She was so quiet it was almost worrisome.

"Go play with Melvin," I said when she was done. "Go on," I said, smiling when she stared at me. "It'll be okay." I knew that Mom wouldn't agree to go to Vegas on such short notice. Mom needed things planned out.

I was just putting the last of the leftovers in the refrigerator when Dad and Mom came into the kitchen. They both had light jackets on. Mom looked a lot calmer, but she didn't have any make-up on.

"We'll be back in an hour, I think, maybe an hour and a half," Dad said lightly.

"Where are you going?"

"Your back to school night."

"Oh," I blinked. I had completely forgotten about it.

Mom was opening the door to the garage. "We said good-night to Grete. Make sure she's in bed on time." She looked over her shoulder at me. "Is there anything you want to tell us before we go meet your teachers?"

"Like which class has the cute boys?" Dad asked, winking at me.

"I was thinking about any problems we should know about

ahead of time," Mom said.

"Silke doesn't have any problems, right Silk?" He ushered Mom out the door. "Don't forget to think of something new to do," he said, as he pulled the door shut behind him. "We'll be back soon."

After I locked all the doors and windows, I checked on Grete; she was sitting on the floor, happily letting Melvin climb all over her. "Think I can take Melvin on my sleep over this weekend?" she asked.

"I don't know," I said. "Don't forget to wash your hands before you brush your teeth."

"Okay!"

I gently closed my bedroom door. I knew that the only way the magic hat could truly be magic would be if I followed the spirit of it. So I had to try something completely different, something completely unexpected. The question was, what?

I picked up my planner and double-checked that I had finished all of my assignments. Mr. Norton had mentioned a possible quiz, but I thought my notes were pretty complete. If I reviewed them quickly during lunch, I'd be fine. But thinking of Western Civ made me think of Dominic.

I could call Dominic.

That would be different.

That would be completely unexpected—unbelievable, even. I tried to picture Alexi's face if I told her I had called the veritable rainbow, but I couldn't do it. She would never believe me. I could hardly believe I was thinking about it myself.

I sat down and ran through what I was going to say a couple of times. Then I got a drink of water and took a deep breath, and called him.

"Yo."

"Is Dominic there?" I asked, though I was sure it was his deep rumble that had answered the phone.

"You got him. Who's this?"

"Silke. From Western Civ."

He snorted. "Thanks for clearing that up. I thought you might be the Silke from science or maybe the one from auto shop."

I didn't say anything. I had called to be nice and he was being a jerk.

"So," he said finally into the silence, "What's up?"

The words wanted to stick in my throat, but I made myself say them anyway. "You haven't been in class lately."

"How sweet! You missed me!"

I was so glad that I was on the phone and not on Skype or sitting in front of him. My face was on fire. "No. I just…."

"Missed me?" He said softly.

"Wondered if you had dropped the class."

"No. I'll be back."

"When?" I asked before I could stop myself.

"See? You do miss me."

"Whatever," I snapped. "See ya."

"Wait—"

But I slapped my phone shut and tossed it on my desk.

Two seconds later it rang again. "Yeah, right," I said to the phone as it flashed his name. "Like I'm going to talk to you now."

I went to put Grete to bed, and had a hard time convincing her that Melvin would rather sleep in his cage.

"What if I put his cage on my bed?" Grete asked as she gently shut the lid.

"He'd be much happier on top of your dresser," I said, moving the cage. "You move around too much and you might knock the cage off."

"I wouldn't!"

"Not on purpose," I said, "Just while you're sleeping. Go wash your hands."

"I already did."

"And then you picked up Melvin. Go wash them again."

I flopped back on Grete's bed, staring at the ceiling while I waited for her. Why had I called Dominic? Why? Even I found him attractive in a strange way, why would I pick him to be the first boy I ever called?

"Yeah, she's here," Grete's voice came from the hall. I sat up. Who was she talking to?

She padded into her room, holding my cell phone to her ear.

"What do you think you're doing?" I demanded.

"It was ringing," she said, holding it out to me.

"Get in your PJs," I growled.

I waited until I was in the hall to look at the display. Of course it was Dominic. I thought about shutting the phone again, but then I took a deep breath and said "Hello?"

"Silke?" His voice rumbled through the cell phone.

"Yes."

"I'm sorry. Sincerely."

"Whatever."

"I mean it."

"It's no big deal."

"Really."

"It's fine," I said, exasperated.

"Was that your little sister?"

"Yeah."

"She sounds cute."

"She is."

There was an uncomfortable silence.

"Well," he said finally, "I'll let you go."

"Okay."

"See you in class."

"If you ever come back."

"Oh, don't worry," he said, chuckling, "I'm coming back."

"Bye."

"Good-night," he said softly, and it was like he was standing next to me. Goosebumps broke out on my arms.

The second time I had to go take Melvin's cage off Grete's bed, I warned her that I would take him into my room if she couldn't leave him alone. From her terrified look, I was certain she didn't know I was bluffing. There was no way I was sleeping with a rodent in my room. I thought about putting Melvin in Mom and Dad's room and laughed.

Mom and Dad came home about twenty minutes after Grete finally fell asleep. I had taken a chance and logged on to Facebook for five minutes, just checking on how everyone was doing. My friends had sent me virtual flowers, two new fish for my reef, and a biscuit for my virtual poodle, so I felt pretty good. I hadn't been forgotten.

"Hi, honey," Dad said, coming into my room.

"Hi."

"Everyone had really nice things to say about you."

"Especially Mr. Norton," Mom added, making me blink. "He's very impressed that you've been so helpful to a student who's going through some serious issues at home."

"Oookaaay."

"And Mrs. Fedderson will be sending home the fundraising information next week."

"You mean I can go?" I asked, hardly daring to breathe.

"We'll see how your grades are and how much money you can raise." Before I could get over my shock, she continued, "And I talked to Alexi's mom. You'll go to her house tomorrow after school."

"I will?"

"And Grete will go to Jilly's. Mrs. Childers signed up to take care of Melvin—"

"On purpose," Dad added with a grin.

Mom shot Dad a look as she continued, "So they're fine taking Melvin as well. Mrs. Childers said Jilly was disappointed not to get Melvin this weekend, so it actually works out well for everybody." Mom shook her head. "I still can't believe Mitchell's already a senior," she said, referring to Jilly's big brother.

"It was fate running into Mrs. Childers at back to school night," Dad said gravely. Then he winked at me.

"Wait, does this mean you're going to Vegas?"

"We're going to Vegas!" Dad said.

"Only if we can get tickets, and that's not very likely," Mom added, sounding almost optimistic.

"Getting tickets, getting tickets right now," Dad said, giving me a quick kiss on the forehead and leaving my room.

"You're going to Vegas," I repeated. I was stunned.

"Dad's wanted to go for a long time," she said. "I know there are some good deals going on right now for airfare and hotels."

"Oh." I still couldn't believe it.

"You and Alexi are not to come over here this weekend," Mom said sternly.

"Am I supposed to take all of my stuff to school with me tomorrow?" I asked, fully expecting her to say yes.

To my surprise, Mom frowned, then said slowly, "You may come get your stuff after school tomorrow, and then you are not to come back till after school on Monday."

"Okay."

"I'm very serious about this, Silke."

"I know."

"Maybe we shouldn't go."

Even though I knew that last bit was more her talking to herself than to me, I pointed out, "Dad's buying tickets right now."

"Maybe I can stop him." She turned on her heel and left.

But Dad had already bought the non-refundable, non-changeable, last minute tickets. The flight left at six the next morning, and they'd fly home Monday at noon.

I had to listen to Mom go over the rules for another twenty minutes, which was irritating since it all boiled down to her not trusting me to stay at home alone. She went over how I was supposed to get Grete with all her stuff to Jilly's tomorrow morning before school and come back for my stuff after school.

"Here's sixty dollars," Mom said, "Janet mentioned taking you and Alexi to the mall and maybe a movie."

"Thanks," I said, feeling overwhelmed.

"You'll have to get up early tomorrow to get everything done," she reminded me.

"I know."

"Make sure you lock everything before you leave."

"I know." I reminded myself that listening to her right now was so worth it. I was going to spend the whole weekend with Alexi!

"Don't lock the keys in the house!"

"I won't!"

"Teresa," Dad said from the hall, "Let Silke get some sleep. We need to pack and get some rest too. We'll have to leave for the airport by three-thirty."

"I can't believe we're doing this," Mom said, shaking her head as she left my room. "I thought the hats were another week away, at least."

*   *   *

When I saw Alexi waiting for me the next morning, I actually started skipping. I quit before I reached her, though, because she was barely smiling.

"Are you all right?"

"I'm not feeling that great," she said with a shake of her head as she turned and fell in step with me.

She didn't look that good, either, looking almost whiter than the sweatshirt she had on. But I kept that thought to myself. "Maybe you should stay home today," I said.

"Can't," she said, shifting her backpack strap. "Quiz in Spanish and first essay due in English. I stayed up till midnight finishing it."

"You shouldn't have done that." She always kept things till the last minute. When she rolled her eyes at me, I pointed out, "They let you make up work if you're sick. You should go back to bed."

She shook her head again. "I'm sorry I'm sick."

"Why? Did you do it on purpose?"

"You're spending entire the weekend with me, and I'm not going to want to do anything."

"So we spend it watching movies, surfing the net and eating chicken noodle soup. We'll still have fun. Just don't give it to me—I hate being sick!"

Alexi gave me a weak smile. "I'll try not to swap germs with you."

"That's what makes you such a great friend!"

By the time we got to school, her face wasn't nearly as pale—instead, she was really flushed. The morning air was pleasantly crisp, but not enough to give her those rosy cheeks and forehead.

Alexi made it through English with me, and she finished the Spanish quiz. She asked to go to the office as soon as she was done, though. As she gathered her things, I tried to catch her eye, but she never looked my way and almost ran from the room.

At lunch, the boys didn't show up. Emma told me that someone in her painting class said they saw Alexi puke in the office.

The rest of the day slid by without any sight of Alexi, and suddenly I was on my way to Western Civ. After a week of school, I felt much more comfortable walking to class alone. Still, I was looking forward to catching up to Bridget and Daisy.

"Forgiven?" a deep voice said at my shoulder.

"I told you—"

"No," Dominic said, matching his stride to mine, "You blew off my sincere apology. I was hoping that—"

"You're forgiven," I interrupted, trying to get rid of him. People were looking at us. Today his hair was parted to show off all the green on one side and yellow on the other.

"Truly?" He half-stepped in front of me as he turned to our classroom door, so we were facing each other and he forced me to stop. His green eyes, a brighter color than his hair, were locked on mine. "Sincerely?"

I sighed. I was going to be late. Before I could say anything, though, he rushed on.

"It was cool that you called me to check on me. I was a jerk. I really am sorry."

"Sincerely?"

"Most sincerely," he said, bowing his head just slightly.

"You are most sincerely forgiven," I said, smiling in spite of myself.

"You both need to get inside, or you'll be marked tardy," Mr. Norton said from his post inside the door. "Sincerely."

CHAPTER SIX

I snapped my phone shut and stared out at the empty parking lot. I had called Alexi's phone three times and her house number twice, but all I had gotten was voice mail. I didn't know her mom's cell number, and I wasn't sure what to do.

Back inside the nearly deserted building, I went to the office.

"Can I help you?" asked Mrs. Shive, the school secretary.

"I was wondering if anyone left a message for me."

"And you are?"

"Silke Reichard," I said, feeling lame.

She shook her head.

"I was supposed to go home with Alexi Amerman," I felt compelled to add.

Mrs. Shive sort of grimaced and shook her head. "She went home sick this morning, that's all I can tell you."

"Okay," I said. "Thanks.

I stopped just outside the doors to check the parking lot again. Still empty. With a sigh, I hitched my backpack up a little higher. The door behind me opened, but before I could turn around, a rich voice asked, "Everything okay?"

"Why are you always coming up behind me?"

"Guess you're a hard person to keep up with."

I rolled my eyes and started down the sidewalk. Dominic fell in step beside me.

"Everything okay?" he asked again.

"Fine."

"Going home?"

"Yeah."

"Cool."

We kept walking. I waited until we had taken about a dozen steps together before I stopped and turned to him. "Where are you going?"

He shrugged. "Don't know."

I stared at him. He just stood there, wind swirling his hair and revealing the multicolored locks, staring right back at me. Waiting.

"What?" I snapped.

He blinked and shrugged again. "Nothin'."

"Where'd your lip ring go?"

"Enh," he shrugged, "Decided I didn't like it."

"Bet your parents decided you didn't like it."

A strange look crossed his face briefly, then he grinned. "No, they didn't care one way or another. But your mom didn't like it at all. And since you called last night—"

"Don't even pretend you got rid of it because of my mother."

"Oh, no. I do things or don't do things simply because I want to, not because of what other people think."

I turned and started walking again, and he was right with me. I tugged at my pack, and did my best to ignore him. He seemed to be slouching along, but he kept up with my quick pace. We were nearly at a corner, though, and I focused on the hope that he would go in a different direction when we reached it.

Instead, he crossed the street with me. On the other side, I stopped again, hands on my hips. "Where do you think you're going?" Standing face to face with him now, I realized that he was bigger than I had thought he was. He wasn't really tall— only about four or five inches taller than me—but he was solid. It was hard to tell if it was muscle or pudginess under the flannel, but as lean as his face was, I guessed it was muscle.

"I'm just walking."

"Could you walk somewhere else?"

"Don't really have anywhere to go," he said. "Thought I'd keep you company, since your friend's not here."

"My fr—what—what do you mean?" I sputtered.

"You usually walk home with that other girl."

"Have you been watching me?"

"I'm observant," he said. "I notice things."

"Like what?

"Like she was pretty sick this morning." I stared at him as he continued blandly, "I thought maybe I'd walk you home."

"Did you ever consider *asking*?"

"You'd rather walk alone?" He asked with what seemed to be genuine surprise.

I opened my mouth but then snapped it shut. How could I answer that without being a total witch?

"You called me last night," he continued. "And I thought... thought that....." He trailed off, looking uncomfortable for the first time.

"I just called....called because...." I didn't know how to finish.

"Sorry," he said abruptly, swinging around. He had taken four big slouching steps back across the street before I found my voice.

"I called because I thought you might need to see my notes again."

He stopped. "It would help."

"Do you want to copy them now?"

Standing there in the middle of the street, he said, "If it's okay."

"Yeah."

"You're sure?"

"Yeah."

He was still standing in the street. A car was slowing down as it approached.

"Sincerely," I said in exasperation.

He grinned. "Okay," and he slouched off the street toward me.

It felt weird, unlocking the front door. I mean, I barely knew him. He seemed harmless, but he was also kind of freaky. And no one else was home. No one else would be coming home, either, at least not for a few days.

But he doesn't know that, I reminded myself. *And I'm sure not going to tell him.*

I took him straight to the kitchen, and felt relieved when he sat at the table without saying anything.

We opened our packs, and I pulled out my notes as he dug and found some crumpled papers. While he began writing, I got a bag of carrots out of the fridge. When I turned to take them to him, I realized how geeky I was being. I put the carrots back and grabbed a couple of sodas and a bag of chips instead.

"Thanks," he said when I set them on the table.

Almost as soon as I sat down at the table, I jumped back up so I could turn on the kitchen radio.

Once again I sat down and then stood up again.

"Am I making you nervous?" he rumbled, not looking up for the notes he was scratching.

"No," my voice squeaked higher than normal and I cleared my throat. "No," I said more clearly. "I just keep forgetting things."

He shook his head but continued writing. Behind the kitchen counter, I tried to find justification for having gotten up again. He *did* make me nervous, but I could scarcely admit it to him. Once again I opened the refrigerator, but there was nothing else that I wanted or needed in there. As I closed the door, something silvery on the counter caught my eye. Dad's cell phone.

I opened Dad's phone, and checked through his contact list. He didn't have Mrs. Amerman's cell phone number, which didn't surprise me. If anyone was going to have Mrs. Amerman's cell number, it would be Mom. I realized I was running out of options. I tried calling one more time.

Both the Amerman house phone and Alexi's cell phone went straight to voice mail.

With a sigh, I called Mom's phone. There really wasn't anything else to do. I was really surprised when it went to voice mail. I was debating what kind of message to leave when movement at the table caught my attention. Dominic was stuffing his papers back in his bag.

Distracted, I hung up. Mom would call back as soon as she saw she had missed my call, anyway. I could figure out what to say then. "Done already?"

He shook his head, not looking at me.

"Is something wrong?"

"I'm making you uncomfortable," he said. "I'll go."

"Finish the notes," I said.

He swung to look at me, and I was startled at how morose his face looked. "I'll go."

"Don't," I said, and surprised myself by adding, "Please."

He looked almost as startled as I was. Slowly he sat back down.

"I—" My phone rang in my hand, and I jumped. Worse than that, I shrieked.

"Oh," I said, putting my hand on my chest. "Oh." I tried to smile at him. He stared back with the same startled expression. My phone rang again, and this time I answered it. "Hello?"

"Silke? It's Janet Amerman." She sounded totally frazzled.

"Hi—" I turned around so I wouldn't have to see Dominic staring at me.

"I'm so sorry about all this," she said.

"It's okay," I replied instantly, though I didn't know what she was sorry for or if it was okay. "How's Alexi feeling?"

Mrs. Amerman gave a short bark of laughter that sounded stressed. "She's out of surgery now—"

"Surgery?" I echoed weakly.

"Yes, her appendix, this morning she wasn't feeling well, and by the time I picked her up from school she had a fever and was vomiting and I took her to the doctor and they sent us right to the hospital and they admitted her and finished the surgery about an hour ago and we'll be here for—for a few more hours, at least."

"Wow," I said. Mrs. Amerman was seriously stressed.

"I'm so sorry that I haven't called before now. I just saw that you called Alexi's phone, and I'm sorry, but I forgot all about—"

"It's okay," I said soothed. "No big deal. I understand." I wanted her to calm down. She was going a million miles a minute. "I'm fine."

"I don't know when I'll be coming home—"

"It's all right. I'll call Emma and see if I can stay with her instead."

"Are you sure?" she said doubtfully, but I could hear relief in her voice too.

"Yes, no problem. I'm sure she'll say yes."

"I ought to call your mother—"

"I just called her a few minutes ago," I said quickly. "When she calls me back, I'll let her know what's going on. I'll stay with Emma. Or Bridget," I added. "I'm sure I can find someone."

"I need to talk to a parent," Mrs. Amerman fretted, "And make sure it's okay."

"Sure," I said. "I'll call you when I get this sorted out and you can talk to a parent."

She gave a big heavy sigh. "I feel awful about this. I told your mom it'd be okay. Alexi was so excited when I told her what was going on—"

"No one knew Alexi was going to get appendicitis," I said. "It's hardly your fault."

"Be sure to call me."

"I will," I promised. "I'll call in….a half-hour, okay?"

"Okay. Sooner if there's a problem."

"Okay. Tell Alexi I hope she feels better soon."

Mrs. Amerman did that bark-laugh again. "She's still under anesthesia, but I'll tell her when she wakes up."

We said good-bye and hung up. I set my phone down. What was I going to do now? I should call Mariel or Emma and see if I could stay with them. I should call someone. Mom would want me to stay with someone, even with someone she hadn't met, like Daisy or Bridget, instead of staying home alone.

"Everything okay?" His rich voice was right behind me

again.

I turned. Dominic had come over to the kitchen island and was standing on the other side. I leaned forward, and he mirrored me.

"Alexi. Appendicitis."

He winced. "Ouch."

"I was supposed to stay with her this weekend."

"But now you're going to Emma's."

I knew he hadn't been trying to eavesdrop and that I hadn't been trying to keep my voice down on the phone, but still, it annoyed me that he didn't at least pretend not to know what was going on.

"Want me to walk you over there?"

"No," I said, shaking my head. "That's all right."

He nodded his head. His hair had gone back to the part he had at school, and the green locks framing his face made his eyes look almost emerald.

"Are you done with the notes?"

He shrugged. "Got most of them." I looked at him and he sighed. "I'll finish 'em up."

He went back to the table. I stayed at the island, leaning on my forearms, trying to think. I shouldn't have been thinking anything. I should have been calling Emma, then Mariel, then Daisy, and then Bridget to see if I could stay with one of them. There shouldn't have been any other thought in my mind.

But there was.

I could stay by myself.

I was never home alone. I was either watching Grete, or Mom or Dad or both of them were home. I was *never* alone. And suddenly I wanted to be alone. No. I needed to be alone. I could prove how responsible I could be by myself. I might not get another chance before I turned eighteen.

Staying home alone would be trying something new.

Once again, Dominic was stuffing papers into his pack.

"Done," he said when he saw me staring at him. "I'll get out of your hair now."

"Why do you do that?"

"Do what?"

"Your hair?"

He stared at me as if I were crazy, and I realized that it probably seemed like I had brought it up out of nowhere, but they were his words, not mine. "Why do you have so many colors in your hair?"

Dominic grinned. "Haven't found the one I like yet."

"Oh."

"You haven't either," he said.

"What?"

"Your hair doesn't have color at all. Have you tried any?"

"My hair has color," I objected.

He raised his eyebrows. "It's not transparent, but it's almost translucent."

I frowned at him, mostly because I couldn't argue the point.

"I think…" he tilted his head to one side and studied me. "I think you'd look good with a dark red."

"I like my color just fine," I lied. I had always wanted to be a redhead, but I had never told anyone that, not even Alexi. Mom would kill me if I did anything like that.

"Suit yourself." He was walking out the kitchen toward the living room and front door before I registered that he was leaving.

"Wait!"

He swung back around, somehow looking slow, but his pack swung out away from him in response to the sharpness.

"Do me a favor?"

"What kind of favor?"

"Make a phone call."

"To who?"

"Alexi's mom."

"The one in the hospital?"

"Yeah."

"What for?"

He was still standing in the middle of the living room,

halfway to the front door. I waved him back to me, and when he started walking, I picked up my phone, tapping it nervously on the counter top. Was I really going to do this?

"Why do you want me to call her?" He asked as he dropped his pack on the floor.

"I want…" my mouth was dry and I had to stop and try to swallow without spit. "I want you to pretend to be Bridget's dad."

"Who's Bridget?"

"A friend," I said. I had decided on Bridget because she was a friend who was new to both Alexi and me, and our parents hadn't met each other yet. "I want you to say that I'm going to stay with you this weekend."

He gave me a mischievous grin. "You're staying with me? All weekend? All right!"

"Dominic," I pleaded, fighting the flush I could feel creeping up my cheeks. "Please? Just call and say you're Mr. Ulbricht, and that it's okay for me to stay with Bridget this weekend."

"What's my name?"

"Mr. Ulbricht?" I said uncertainly, because I wondered if he was checking to see if I knew who he was.

"Duh. First name."

I blinked. "I dunno."

"I need to know the dude's first name."

"Why?"

He leaned forward on the counter. "Do you want to get away with this? 'Cause if you do, you gotta do it right. If you want to get caught," he pulled a phone out of his pocket. "I'll just cruise through it right now."

"I don't know Bridget's dad's name," I said, reaching out and putting my hand over his phone so he couldn't start dialing. Which was stupid, really, because he didn't have the phone number yet.

Dominic's green eyes were almost magnetic. "Let's find out," he said.

"How?"

He rolled his eyes and pulled his hand away from mine. I put both my hands behind my back. "Start with a phone book," he said. "How many Ulbricht's can there be?"

Not many, as it turned out. Three were listed, but two had the same address, in our zip code. The other entry was across town from us. "William Ulbricht."

"William Ulbricht," Dominic said, his voice rolling like soft thunder. "William Ulbricht, William Ulbricht." He nodded. "Got it. What else do I need to know?"

I shrugged helplessly. "You're Bridget's dad, we have Western Civ together—"

"Wait, which one's Bridget?"

"What?" I stared at him blankly.

"She sits in front of you in Western Civ?"

"Yeah."

"Is she the really tall one or the really scrawny one?"

"I, uh—" I had to think. "She's taller than Daisy," I said. I didn't consider Bridget really tall or Daisy really scrawny, but in comparison to each other—"She's the one with the long brown hair," I added.

Dominic nodded, frowning in concentration. He lifted his hand so his thumb was at his ear and his pinky in front of his mouth, the classic hand phone. "William Ulbricht here, M— who's Alexi's mom?"

"Mrs. Amerman."

"First name?" There was a touch of impatience in his voice.

"Janet. Janet Amerman."

He nodded again. "William Ulbricht here. May I speak to Janet Amerman?"

I grinned. "Brill—"

He waved a hand at me. "Bridget's just told me what's going on. We'd be happy to—" He broke off again. "Are her parents married?"

I shrugged helplessly.

He looked disgusted, but went back to talking into his pinky. "—We'd be happy to have Silke stay with us for the weekend.

You've got plenty to deal with. I hope Alexi recovers quickly."

"Wow," I said, but he waved at me again and I shut up. He ran through his part of the conversation four or five more times, not stumbling at all on the last two runs.

"Ready," he said, grabbing his phone with his phony hand and flipping it open.

"Wait! What are you doing?" I grabbed for his hand again.

"Thought you wanted me to—"

"Use my phone," I said. "I'll call her and then hand you the phone."

"Were you not listening to me?" he demanded. "If you're making the call, why do I need to ask for her?"

"I, uh—" I closed my mouth and then tried again, "I thought—"

"Just give me the number," he said, sounding tired.

"I don't have her number."

He slapped his phone shut again. "What?"

"I have Alexi's number, not hers."

Dominic rolled his eyes again. "Whatever. I'm going to ask for the mom anyway. Just give me the number."

I did, and as he punched the last number, he turned so he was staring at the photo of Grete and me that Mom had taken last year at the corn maze, and held out his hand, palm up, toward me. "Not a sound!"

I took a step back, leaned against the oven, and covered my mouth with both hands.

After a few seconds, I was sure it was going to go to voice mail. I lowered my hands. "I thin—"

He snapped and pointed at me without turning his head. "William Ulbricht here, trying to reach Janet Amerman. I know you're very busy right now with your daughter, and I just wanted to let you know that we're happy to have Silke stay here with Bridget for the weekend. Please don't worry about a thing, but if you need to reach me, my number's 555-2383. We all hope Alexi recovers quickly. Good-bye."

He closed his phone and then he finally turned to look at me, grinning. I was staring at him, bug-eyed, both hands still over my mouth. Otherwise, I would have screamed at him.

"What?"

I shook my head. I was afraid to move my hands.

"I don't even get a thank you?"

"What?" I screeched. "When you just left her *your* phone number? How could you do something so stupid?"

"That doesn't sound like thank you."

"Dominic, you just—"

"Left my phone number on a phone that was going to log my number anyway."

I swallowed. I hadn't even thought of that.

"And by voluntarily leaving my number, it decreases the chance that she'll want to call back."

"Thank you," I said meekly.

He inclined his head. "You're welcome."

I let out a big sigh I didn't know I'd been holding. Free. I was free for a whole weekend. No one to watch, no one to worry about, no one to ask permission. I could be me—maybe even find out who I really was. I was free.

"You know what this means, right?"

I looked at him and felt the big grin on my face slip just a little.

"You owe me." He bent down and picked up his pack. "You owe me *big*."

My stomach clenched as he took two steps along the island, but then he turned toward the living room and front door and I relaxed a little.

"Thank you," I said again. "Sincerely."

When he reached the front door, he turned around and smiled. "You're sincerely welcome." He opened the door. "But you still owe me."

"Wait! What does that mean?"

Dominic raised his eyebrows and his smile turned to a smug grin. "We'll figure that out later." He pulled the door shut behind him.

CHAPTER SEVEN

I had a blast. I had no idea being in a house alone could be so much fun!

First off, I made myself a giant ice cream sundae, complete with whipped cream, chocolate syrup, and two cherries. And I drank a Coke with it. We have sweets around the house, but Mom rations them out like she's afraid the stores will stop making them and we'll never get anymore. The ice cream lid had a thick layer of ice crystals, and the last time I remember anyone using the chocolate syrup was when Grete had chocolate milk on the Fourth of July.

Then I went in the living room, and cranked the stereo. I cranked it up so high, in fact, that I could feel the bass thumping in my stomach. I ran back to my room, and grabbed three of my favorite CDs and took them back to the living room. I wanted my music loud, not their light 70's and 80's station loud. After two songs, I turned the volume down so it was loud but bearable.

I danced around the living room, and somehow found myself jumping from the couch to the love seat and back again until I was exhausted and I belly-flopped on the sofa and lay there, panting.

The music was pulsing through the speakers in rhythm with my heart. I felt so good, so free. The house was peaceful; I could feel it even with the music booming. No one was disappointed, no one was angry, no one was putting their needs or wishes behind someone else's—it was calm and easy.

When I got up to change the CD, I decided it was time to start thinking about dinner. Nothing in the fridge really appealed to me. It was Friday night and I was having my own private party. That meant pizza! After all, Mom had left money for me.

When I called to order, the really nice guy asked if I wanted to add hot wings, a two liter bottle of Coke, and an order of cherry pie pizza, for an extra $9.99, and I said sure. Why not?

I ran back to my room and put on make-up, using more than Mom liked to see on me, and then put on a really cute short skirt that Alexi had leant me a month ago and I had never found a chance to wear. I tried putting my hair up and decided I didn't like it, but when I let it down again, it had a nice tousled look to it, so I left it. *A little unkempt tonight*, I thought, *that's me*.

The doorbell rang and I ran back to the front door, snagging the money I had set on the dresser as I went. Two feet from the door, I skidded to a stop. Very loudly, seemingly right in my ear, I heard my mother say, "What do you think you're doing? You NEVER open the door without checking to see who it is! At least use *some* of the brains I know you have!"

Obediently I put my eye to the peephole. A pizza delivery girl, loaded down with my pizza, wings, dessert and drink, was waiting.

After we exchanged the food for the money, she turned to go. "Hope you and your friends have fun," she said as she left.

"Wha—Thank you," I stammered, realizing that it must look like I was having a party with my friends. As I shut the door with my hip, suddenly my private party didn't seem quite as cool as it had.

I almost took the food to the kitchen before I decided that was really stupid. I did a heel turn that would have landed me on my face if anyone else had been watching, but because I was alone, it was perfect. I set the food in the middle of the living room floor, and grabbed two pillows off the couch.

It took me a minute to find the remote; Grete must have had it last, and she was lucky I found it. Mom would have yelled at her if she had been the one to discover the remote was not in its designated space.

Once again I started to sit, but stopped again. Darkness was falling. I turned on the living room and kitchen lights, and then went around checking all the doors and windows. Not because it was what I was supposed to do, but because I was suddenly a little freaked about being in the house by myself.

I gorged on the pizza and wings, and had to put the cherry pie pizza in the fridge for later. I drank the soda right out of the bottle, and ended up belching for five minutes straight. It took nearly twenty minutes of channel surfing before I found a movie I wanted to watch. It was from last winter, and it was finally on cable. It was also rated R, which would give Mom a hissy fit, and was more than twice the amount of TV I was allowed to watch each day—when I wasn't grounded from watching TV, which, technically, I still was.

I caught up with everyone on Facebook, but didn't tell anyone what I was doing. Mom had my password, and could check all my posts and conversations whenever she wanted to. But Alexi and I frequently got on Facebook at her house together, so my posts tonight wouldn't look odd. I played a few of my games too, and a couple more hours had passed before I knew it.

After I brushed my teeth and got into a pair of old sweats, I took the comforter off my bed and took it to the living room. It took me a little longer to find a movie this time, but that was all right.

I fell asleep on the couch with the TV and lights on.

The ringing of the doorbell woke me.

Disoriented, I blinked as I looked around the living room, not immediately recognizing where I was. The TV was still on, showing a movie from a couple of years ago. The cable box clock said 8:12. I had spent the night in the living room. My private party had turned into a private slumber party.

The doorbell rang again.

I rolled off the couch, dragging my blanket with me, as the doorbell rang yet again.

"Coming," I muttered, though not loud enough for anyone on the other side of the door to hear. "Who's here at eight on a

Saturday morning, anyway?"

I kind of ran into the door as I went to put my eye to peephole.

Immediately the doorbell rang three times in a row. "Come on, Silke," Dominic said, now pounding on the door I was leaning against. "I know you're in there!"

I had to pull my eye back from the peephole because suddenly his eye was on the other side.

"What are you doing?" I yelled through the door.

"Collecting. Open up."

"Collecting what?"

"The IOU. Open the door!" He rang the doorbell four more times.

"Okay, okay, okay," I said, "Just stop it!"

I fumbled with the lock for a moment, and Dominic leaned on the doorbell, creating one painfully long ring.

By the time I yanked the front door, what little cheerful morning feelings I had even on a good day were gone. "Stop it already!" I snarled.

"Not much of a morning person, huh?" He said with a big smile as he walked right in. "Here. Maybe this will help."

He shoved a Styrofoam cup into my hand. The pungent smell of coffee filled my nostrils.

"What are you doing?" I asked, following as he headed toward the kitchen.

"Got breakfast." He held up a take-out caddy holding another Styrofoam cup and a small paper bag. "Coffee and jelly-filled donuts. The breakfast of champions."

I stared at him. He sat down at the kitchen table. "You can say thank you anytime now."

It was sweet, and at a different time, I would have been saying thank you as soon as he handed me the coffee. But it was eight o'clock in the morning, I had been up late last night, and I hadn't invited him over. "What are you doing here?"

"I told you," he said, pulling a donut out of the bag. "I'm collecting that IOU."

I stared at him. He bit into his donut and then took a sip of coffee. "Damn," he said, "Careful, it's still pretty hot."

I glared at him.

"I thought I should come and check on you," he said, leaning back from the table. "Especially since I just assured Janet that you were fine."

"You what?"

"I told Janet Amerman that you and Bridget had a great time last night, but had stayed up kind of late, so you couldn't talk to her just then. I promised I'd have you call when you woke up." He held his phone out toward me, smiling.

"She called this morning?"

"I'm not usually up this early," he said dryly.

"Oh, thank you, thank you, thank you," I whispered, sitting down on the chair.

"You ought to call her," he said, setting the phone on the table and sliding it over to me. "She seemed a little concerned." He took the lid off his coffee cup and blew the steam off.

I nodded.

He took another bite of donut. Some of the jelly squirted out on the side of his mouth and he wiped it off with the tip of his pinky finger.

"What did you tell her? What did she say?"

"I told you. I said you and Bridget were sleeping in and that you'd call her when you wake up."

"That's it?"

"That's it. But it took me twenty minutes to get here," he added when I didn't move.

I looked at his phone. It was battered and scratched, and probably at least three years old.

"It won't bite," he said.

"I'll get my phone in a minute."

"Suit yourself," he said, "But you should use mine."

"Why?"

"To make it look like you're really at my—Bridget's—

house."

"You've done this a lot, haven't you?"

He waggled his eyebrows. "Of course. All I do is cause trouble."

I reached for his phone, but he cleared his throat. "What?"

"Take a drink of coffee, and then a deep breath."

Ignoring the coffee, I inhaled deeply, and held it for a moment. Then I picked up his phone and dialed Alexi's number.

"Alexi's phone," her mom said.

"Hi, Mrs. Amerman."

"Silke, how are you?"

"I'm good. How's Alexi doing?"

Mrs. Amerman made a clicking noise with her tongue. "Well, the surgery went fine, but they're not really happy with her recovery. She's having trouble keeping food down, so they're keeping her a little longer, but hopefully I can bring her home this afternoon."

"That's too bad," I said. "I guess I should wait to talk to her."

"She's sleeping right now, so yes, you'll have to wait. I feel so awful about this—"

"Please don't," I said. "It's not like you made Alexi get sick or anything...is it?"

She laughed just like I wanted her to. "No, this was certainly not part of my plan. But are you and Bridget all right?"

"Everything's good," I assured her.

"I should probably call your parents," she said, and I wondered what it was about parents that made them want to have the same conversations over and over.

"Dad left his cell phone here," I told her, "And Mom's not answering her phone."

"Yes, but I think they told me the hotel they're staying at....I have it written down at home."

"They're supposed to be getting away," I pointed out.

"Everything's under control, so why bother them?" She

sighed, and I pushed just a little bit more. "Mr. and Mrs. Ulbricht are fine with me being here, and Mrs. Ulbricht just went out to get something she wants to cook for us for dinner."

"Still, I feel—"

"Do you want to talk to Mr. Ulbricht again?" I asked in desperation. I didn't dare look up, because I didn't want to see Dominic's expression, but something thumped on the table. "He's right here."

"No," she said, "You're right. Everything's under control, and I'm sure your parents would rather enjoy their time than worry about something that's already been taken care of."

"Exactly."

"Call if you need anything," she said.

"Can I call Alexi this afternoon?"

"That should be fine," Mrs. Amerman said. "Thank you for your understanding."

"Sure. Good-bye." I hung up the phone and slid it back across to Dominic before letting my head drop onto the table with a solid thunk.

"You're welcome."

"Thanks."

"Did your parents never teach you manners?"

I turned my head to the side, so I was looking up at him with one eye. "I'm on vacation."

"From good manners?"

I snorted. "I can't believe *you're* scolding *me* for manners."

"What's that supposed to mean?"

I shook my head.

"Let's see," he said, ticking points off on his fingers, "I've walked you home, I've done you two favors, I've brought you breakfast, I've said please and thank you...I've been nothing but a model of good manners."

I wanted to argue but I couldn't.

"And," he added, "I came to the table dressed."

I glared at him. "I'm dressed."

"In what you slept in."

"Because you came over too early."

"What else was I supposed to do?"

"You could have just called me."

"And what would you have done if Janet wanted to talk to me?"

I snapped my mouth shut against what I wanted to say.

"Aren't you going to eat your donut?"

"You can have it."

"What about your coffee?"

"I'll get to it," I said.

The bag slid across the table to me. "You really should eat breakfast. It's the most important meal of the day."

I pushed myself up from the table and leaned back. "What are you?"

"What do you mean?"

I gestured helplessly. "You act all polite and caring—"

"Who says it's an act?"

"—and you bring food I didn't ask for and get insulted that I'm not excited—"

"Never look a gift horse in the mouth."

"—but you look like an utter freak!"

"I what?"

I was embarrassed, but I refused to look away. "You can't pretend it's an accident," I pressed. "Clearly you want to be a freak."

"Why do you think I'm a freak? Because of my hair?"

"Duh."

"Haven't you ever heard of freedom of expression? Or individualism? Why are you such a conformist?"

"And what is it with the way you talk? You talk like a dictionary! Who really talks like that?" And in my head I heard Alexi telling our lunch group that my word for the week was amok.

He put the last bit of his donut in his mouth. He chewed slowly, swallowed, and then took a sip of coffee. "I think you should go get ready."

"Ready for what?"

"To redeem your IOU."

"Excuse me?"

"It's not a good idea to carry a debt," he said seriously, "It's much better to pay it off right away."

"Exactly what do you want me to do?"

"You'll see."

"I'm not going to agree to just anything," I said, hoping he wouldn't point out the obvious.

"You already did," he said, and I gritted my teeth. "So are you ready to go?"

"No." I stood up from the table. "Stay here."

"Sure," he said.

I walked down the hall, grabbed some clothes from my room, and went to the bathroom. I locked the doorknob, and then tested to make sure it would hold.

Seeing myself in the mirror, I nearly burst into tears. My hair was sticking straight up on one side, the make-up I forgot to take off last night was smeared around my eyes, and I could still see the couch pillow patterns faintly on my red cheek. How bad had they been ten minutes ago, when I answered the door? I had been calling Dominic a freak, and I looked like a total loser.

I showered quickly, completely paranoid that Dominic was going to walk in on me. Why, I don't know. He hadn't shown any interest in me that way. Not that I wanted him to.

Once I was fully dressed, I was able to relax a little. I put my make-up on and fixed my hair. If I took a little bit longer than I normally did to get ready, he wouldn't know.

I put on a pair of comfortable jeans and a favorite shirt. As I passed my bedroom, I resisted the idea of putting Alexi's short skirt back on.

Dominic had moved to the living room and was watching TV. I ignored him as I went to the kitchen and got my phone from its charger. "Where's my coffee?" I called when I saw that he had cleared the table.

"I've got it," he rumbled from behind me, making me jump.

"Ready?" he asked again as he handed me the cup.

I wanted to ask him 'Ready for what?' or say something withering or at least something thought provoking. His green eyes were locked on mine.

"Ready," I said simply, as if I always left the house not knowing where I was going and with a boy I barely knew.

CHAPTER EIGHT

We hardly talked as we walked down the street. I didn't know what he was thinking, but I had decided I was going to be cool and mysterious today. He wasn't going to get the reactions he so clearly liked to provoke from me.

I kept glancing at him out of the corner of my eye. How did he slouch so gracefully? It almost looked like he was gliding. And he was fast! I was using my longest strides trying to keep up with him.

After we got to the main road, Dominic stopped. "Now what?"

"What do you mean?"

"What do you want to do?"

"I thought I was paying back my IOU."

"You are."

"What does that mean?"

Dominic winced as a big truck blew by, tossing dirt and small pebbles on the sidewalk. "Mean's we're going to hang out. What do you want to do?"

I shook my head, trying to make sense of what he was saying. "How does hanging out with you pay you back?"

"It gives me the chance to make up for being a jerk when you called."

"You weren't a jerk."

"Well, I certainly wasn't polite."

I stared at him, and he just looked back at me. I didn't get it. He was so….stoic. Utterly unflappable. I hadn't spent a lot of time with him, but he was never really responsive about anything. "How about we say that the favor you did for me yesterday makes up for not being kind when I called you?"

"Sure."

"Great. So we're even."

"No. You still owe me."

"What?"

"I helped you this morning, too, remember?"

"You're keeping score? Seriously?" He had to be the strangest person on the planet. What had I done to draw his attention like this?

"Well, yeah. I want to be fair," he added earnestly.

"Super."

He looked up and down the street. "Any ideas?"

I held my hands out to either side and shrugged.

"Okay, let's go." He turned and started walking down the street. I had to trot to catch up with him.

"So where are we going?"

"You'll have to wait and see."

"But what if I don't want to go there?"

"You had the chance to pick. You didn't choose, so it's up to me."

"But—"

"Silke, don't you know it's rude to be pushy?"

"You sound just like my mother!"

"You ought to listen to her more often."

I stopped short. "What are you?" I demanded. "You are such a...a...a social misfit!"

He took the two steps that he had continued with to come back to me, and he took my hand as he started walking again. "Yeah. Tell me something I don't know."

It took me a few seconds, but I finally came up with, "That'd be hard to do since you seem to think you know everything."

He glanced at me and grinned.

But he didn't let go of my hand. And I didn't mind.

*　　　　　*　　　　　*

"Are we supposed to be here?"

"The door was open."

"Yeah, but—"

"We haven't broken anything."

"Yeah, but—"

"And I won't let you steal anything."

I pushed him. Not hard or mean, just enough to let him know he was being difficult. I didn't say he was being difficult, because I knew that he already knew it.

We were on the roof of a building. We had gone into a shop on the ground floor, wandered out into a hall and found an elevator, but it was key operated. Dominic didn't give up, however, and wandered a little farther and found an emergency staircase.

"It's going to be locked," I said. "We're not supposed to go up there."

"It's propped open," he replied. "Come on."

So we climbed twelve flights of stairs and that's how we ended up on the roof. A totally crazy roof. It was marked off with paint, making ten rectangles about the size of parking spaces, with a three-foot aisle going down the middle of them. Each parking space, or roof cubicle as Dominic called them, made its own little world.

One was a garden, though most of the planter boxes only had potting soil in them now. There were a few with tomato plants, and one large planter box that was covered with a vine. It had huge leaves, and four or five pumpkins growing on it, but they were still green. One had a half-full kiddie pool, a cooler, and two beach chairs, and one had been lined with astro turf and had two small holes, apparently someone's putting green. Another one had two big clear plastic tubs filled with books, and what appeared to be a recliner wrapped in a tarp. An outdoor reading room on the roof.

Dominic led me right through the roof cubicles to the edge. There was a four-foot brick wall that lined the edge of the roof, which made me feel better. The kiddie pool had made me nervous; the idea of a kid wandering around the roof bothered my mother-instilled sense of safe parenting. But the wall meant that it was relatively safe.

And then Dominic climbed up and sat on it, dangling his feet over the edge.

"What are you doing?" I screeched.

"Checking the view."

"You can do that with your feet over here!" I was standing two feet back from the wall. I wanted to grab him and yank him back onto the roof, but I had a terrifying vision of accidentally pushing instead of yanking and sending him to splat on the asphalt below.

"Come see," he said. "It's cool."

"No."

"Come on, Silke," he said, patting the top of the wall. "It's safe."

"Not until you get off that wall."

"Silke—"

I crossed my arms and shook my head. "I'm going back."

"But you haven't even looked over the edge!"

I took a step backward.

"Okay, okay," he swung his legs back so they were dangling inside the wall instead of outside, which should have made me feel better, except he turned so fast that he leaned back a little, hanging off the roof.

I sprang forward and put both my hands on his knees and put my weight down.

"Whoa!"

I let go of one knee and grabbed his arm, yanking him off the wall, which was fine, but we were both off balance, so we fell in a tangled heap, and that was not so fine.

"Ow-wow-ow," I moaned.

"Yeow! I think I scraped my elbow off!"

I managed to sit up and looked at the knee that had buckled under me. My jeans weren't ripped, but when I pulled them up, I found a decent-sized scrape on my knee and was pretty sure it'd bruise, too.

I glanced over at Dominic. The elbow he said he scraped off

didn't look any worse than my knee did.

"You all right?" he asked.

"Yeah," I said, rolling my jean leg back down.

"No, I mean, are you all right? Why'd you freak out like that?"

"You were hanging over the edge of a twelve-story roof!"

"No," he said, standing up and dusting off his pants. "I was sitting on the edge of the roof. I wasn't hanging over it."

"Still—"

"And if you had gotten close enough to look," he continued as he reached down, grabbed my hand and hauled me to my feet, "The wall is at least a foot wide and there's a three-foot border around it before the edge of the building. It's kind of a false wall."

He pulled me to the wall, and I saw that, surprise, he was right. Looking over the wall didn't even give a good view of the street below; because the roof extended out so far past the wall you couldn't look straight down. I felt foolish. But I wasn't about to admit it.

"Well," he said as we took the elevator back down (you didn't need a key when you were upstairs, apparently), "That wasn't quite what I was expecting." He rubbed his elbow and then stretched it out, grimacing.

I shot him a dirty look but didn't say anything.

Back out on the street, he said, "Now what?"

"We call it a day?"

"It's not even ten yet," he said, then he snapped his fingers. "I know!" And he was slouching off again. It was tempting to stay where I was, to just let him go without me. But evidently the temptation to go with him was stronger, because I found myself trotting after him.

I wish I hadn't.

We took a bus out towards the mall. When we got off at the intersection close to the mall, I thought we were going to the mall. That I could handle. Hanging out at the mall was like second nature to me.

But then I realized it'd be weird to be there with him, and I started to panic. The chances of running into someone I knew were pretty high. How would I explain spending my Saturday morning with the freaky rainbow gone amok?

But before I worked myself into a true tizzy, he was slouching off across the street, away from the mall.

And toward the hardware store.

"What are we doing?" I asked.

"Getting supplies."

"For what?"

"You'll see."

We ended up in the paint section. Well, he did. When I caught up with him (having stopped to look at a cool mirror with a gilt Art-Deco kind of frame. It was in the hardware store! Who knew?), he was already walking toward the registers, carrying four cans of spray paint.

"What's that for?"

"You'll see."

When Dominic set the cans of paint down on the counter, the clerk's eyebrows went up.

"What are those for?" He asked.

I was expecting Dominic to smart off to him too, and was surprised when he said, "School project." I was especially surprised since I didn't know of any projects that required spray paint.

My surprise must have shown on my face, because the clerk clearly did not believe him. "You need a parent to buy these."

"What?"

"We don't sell spray paint to juveniles."

"That's discrimination!"

"It's store policy," the clerk said. "Spray paint can be used for too many bad things."

"Like what?" I demanded, surprising myself. I shouldn't really care, since I had no idea what Dominic wanted to do with the paint, but I got caught up in Dominic's indignation— why weren't kids allowed to buy paint?

"Like making meth. Or tagging."

Well, that calmed me down. I had no idea that spray paint was used to make meth. How stupid was that?

Dominic's indignation, however, seemed to have increased. "You're doing this because of how I look!" His volume had increased too, and people were starting to stare. I wanted to fall through the crack in the cement floor I was standing on.

"I want to see your manager! I'm going to file a complaint with the ACLU! I'm going to sue!"

"What seems to be the problem here?" A lady in a vest materialized at the clerk's counter. Her nametag said, Hi, I'm Mindy! With Store Manager printed underneath, in case there was any confusion.

"I don't like being profiled as a criminal."

"That's not what—" The clerk blustered.

"You're insinuating that because of my age and appearance I'm going to use this product in an illegal manner!" Dominic had lowered his volume, slightly. "That's prejudiced, and infringing on my civil rights!"

"I'm sorry, sir," Mindy said, "But it's corporate policy that minors can only purchase one can of paint at a time. Otherwise—"

"Well, why didn't you just say so?" Dominic said, smiling brightly. "I'll buy this one and she'll buy that one, and you can just put those two back."

"Of course," the manager said, picking up the two cans and gliding away.

Instead of apologizing, the clerk grumbled and glared the whole time he rang up each can of paint—in separate sales to Dominic and me. Dominic, of course, handed me the cash to buy my can.

When Dominic picked up the two bags, he smiled brightly at the clerk and said, "Thank you so much for your help. I hope you have a great day!" as if he hadn't caused a scene three minutes earlier.

He was still smiling as we crossed the parking lot.

"So what was that all about?"

"Hmm?"

"That. Back there."

"Oh, that was just about making sure that people don't peg me. The clerk thought I was an uneducated delinquent. I bet he didn't understand half of what I said."

"Probably not. But why is the paint so important? What are we going to do?"

"Go tagging."

I could not have heard him correctly. "What?"

"I'm going to take you out tagging. Everyone should do a little vandalism once in their lives."

"No they shouldn't!"

"Yeah, they should. It's cool."

"Wrecking someone else's property is so NOT cool!"

He grinned. I should have been angry, I should have been walking away, but somehow that grin made everything different.

"It is cool," he insisted, "When it's done the right way."

The bus pulled up to the bus stop. Dominic took a step forward. When I didn't move, he turned and looked at me.

"I don't think this is a good idea."

"Oh, it's not, don't worry."

"I'm not coming with you."

The change on Dominic's face was almost instant. It went from being calm and happy to looking a lot like Grete did when she dropped a full glass of grape juice on the living room carpet.

"Please?" he said.

"Uh-uh," I said, taking a step back. Lying to my friend's mother about this weekend was dangerous enough. Possibly getting caught vandalizing was too much.

"Are you coming or not?" The bus driver shouted crossly.

Without taking his eyes off me, Dominic shook his head and waved the bus on. The doors hissed as they closed, and the bus belched thick black smoke as it trundled past us.

"Sorry," he said. "I thought maybe it was time to get you out of your comfort zone."

"There's nothing wrong with a comfort zone if you like it," I said.

Another bus pulled up, this one the A25 that ran the route closest to my house. Neither of us said anything as we got on. We didn't say anything on the bus, either. Dominic got up and got off the bus several stops before I would have. I followed him anyway.

I wasn't sure why. He was so confusing. On one hand, he was so smart, talking like a dictionary—like me. On the other hand, he seemed ready for trouble. It was like he didn't know who he was supposed to be. Like me.

We started walking in silence. As we approached the building we had gone roof crashing on, I said, "I'm not going back up there."

"We've already been there. Why go back again?"

"So where are we going?"

"I'm taking you home."

"What?"

"I'm not trying to wreck your day, Silke. I'll walk you home and leave you alone."

At first that made me feel better. But as we kept walking, I liked the new plan less and less. I liked the way I had acted less and less too. He was being imperious, but I was pouting like a brat.

We got to the elementary school and I stopped.

He slouched forward a few more steps before he realized that I wasn't next to him. He stopped and turned around, but he didn't come back to me. "Something wrong?"

"Where are we going?"

"Taking you home," he said as if I was slow.

"We've already been there. Why go back?"

He frowned at me.

"Let's go somewhere else," I said. "Somewhere we both want to go."

"Like where?"

"I don't—

"—know," he finished with me. And we both laughed. I think it was the first time we had laughed together.

"Let's go to the playground," I said.

"The playground?"

"To figure out where we want to go," I said, sensing he didn't really want to go to the playground.

"Okay," he said, and we both turned toward the elementary school together.

I was going to the swings, but he moved toward the merry-go-round. It had been painted in alternating yellow and green pieces of pie when I started school there, but it had enough dirt and rust on it now that it was basically brown all over. He sat in between two of the arched handles; I sat on the other side of one.

"Haven't been on one of these in years."

I didn't say anything.

"Do you come here a lot?"

"Little sister means I come here more than I want to."

"Oh."

We were both pushing with our feet, swaying the merry-go-round side to side instead of letting it go around in one direction.

"So...options," I said. "We could...go to the mall."

He snorted.

"Go tooooo...a museum."

"A museum? And see a bunch of old dead stuff?"

"The art museum?"

"Have you seen the giant upside down purple chair they have in front of it? How is that art?"

"Good point."

"How about an arcade?" he suggested.

"Enh," I said. I hated video games, but at least he was trying now.

"Go karts?"

"Where would we find go karts?"

"Six Flags…closed last week, didn't it?"

"Yep." I could tell it was my turn again. "Go see a movie?"

"Sure," he said, but as I started to feel relieved he added, "I think the first matinees start in about three hours."

"Right. Why isn't there anything to do?"

"Lots to do," he countered. "Just nothing right now that we both want to do."

He suddenly pushed four times with his feet in the same direction, and we began revolving. I wondered why it seemed so easy to just sit with him quietly like this. I liked to talk a lot. Usually I felt weird if someone wasn't talking. But it felt natural to be with Dominic, like I had known him a long time, even though we had just met a couple of weeks ago. And if it hadn't been for the magic hat—

"Bowling!"

"Bowling?" he said doubtfully.

"Yeah," I said. Mom and Dad said they had a lot of fun bowling when the magic hat sent them there.

"I've never bowled."

"Neither have I."

"You suggested it." His tone was almost accusatory.

"My parents just went last week. I've never…well, actually, I think a friend had a birthday party there when we were, like, six."

"I dunno."

"Come on. If neither of us knows what we're doing—"

"We can both make fools of ourselves?"

"Right."

"Okay," and although he still sounded doubtful, he was smiling, "Let's go bowl."

So we did.

And we sucked.

I mean, really, really sucked.

We bowled six frames without either of us hitting a pin. Finally, the old guy who helped us get our shoes and showed us how to set up the computer with our names and even told us that we played in frames and each had two chances to knock down the pins, took pity on us. He came over, gave us the lightest bowling balls, and set up bumpers, so we couldn't get gutter balls. After that we did much better, and Dominic even got a strike.

We bowled three games, stopped and ate hot dogs, nachos, and French fries for lunch, and then bowled two more. By the time we stopped, my arm hurt. But my sides and cheeks hurt even more from all the laughing. We had a great time.

*   *   *

I closed the front door and leaned back against it. No way Cinderella could have felt better than I did right then. It had been such a great day—well, after Dominic quit trying to be a delinquent.

I pulled my phone out of my pocket to call Alexi and examine every minute of the day. Like what did Dominic mean when he said—

"Crap!" I gasped, staring at the phone. Nine missed calls. *Nine*! Somehow I had turned it off. "No, no," I scrolled through the list of missed calls, my heart in my throat. When I got to the last one, I took a deep breath and wiped the sweat off my forehead. Mom hadn't called. Six were from Alexi, two from Bridget, and one from Emma.

I didn't bother with the messages; I hit speed dial and then put the phone to my ear.

"Where are you?" Alexi shouted into the phone.

"I told your mom I'm at Bridget's," I said.

"I know that," Alexi said, annoyed. "But where are you? I called Bridget about an hour ago."

I felt like I had just taken a step that dropped down four feet instead of three inches. "Did your mom talk to her?"

"No, but you should have called Bridget to let her know she was your cover story."

"I can't believe I was so stupid," I said. I thought about what would happen if Mom found out that not only had I spent the night alone at our house, I had also lied to her friend to do it, and I shuddered. "I gotta call Bridget," I muttered. "I'll call you back."

"Silke!" Alexi's voice squawked through the phone as I pulled it from my ear and snapped it shut.

As I dialed Bridget's number, I tried to figure out what I was going to say to her. Too bad Dominic had already gone home; he would certainly be able to tell me what to say.

After bowling, we had gone shopping, but he didn't want to go to the mall. Instead, we went to Wal-Mart. I had no idea how entertaining Wal-Mart could be. We went down the food aisles first, then worked our way through each department.

Looking at the vast array of items that Wal-Mart stocked was only part of the fun, though. People watching was what really entertained us.

The moms cruising with five kids, the dads who were struggling to keep one kid in line, the grandparents who stopped to read the labels on five different types of canned pineapple before picking one, the teens who were checking out the DVDs, the pre-teens who were lagging behind their parents so they didn't look like they were with them....it was a never ending parade of people. And Dominic had stories for all of them.

"Look out!" he pulled me back into the aisle quickly, almost making us both fall. "You've got to look both ways before you cross, or you'll get run over!"

We waited another 40 seconds before the man on the motorized scooter-shopping cart hummed past us.

"Thanks," I said dryly. "He almost flattened me."

"I'm here for you," he said.

Later, in the lingerie section, I left him when he pulled down a monster-sized bra and asked if I thought it would work for making twin sandcastles.

"You're unbelievable," I said while we were scanning to

DVDs. He was improvising a synopsis for a movie called *Beverly's Beauty*.

"What?"

"You're so judgmental."

"It's fun."

"What do you think other people say about you?"

"What ever they want to," he said with a shrug. "But I'm sure it's nothing even close to the truth."

"Oh?"

"Admit it," he said, flashing his emerald eyes at me. "You were sure I was a freaky jerk instead of the ultra-polite and polished young gentleman you now know me to be."

I made gagging noises.

"Admit it," he repeated, poking me with the corner of the DVD case. "I am nothing short of spectacular."

"And modest."

"Always."

I shook my head, but I really couldn't be mad. I was having too much fun.

We left Wal-Mart ("And now you know the real reason the parking lot's always full," Dominic had said as we left. "It has nothing to do with prices. It has to do with people.") and stopped at a little hole-in-the-wall café, which Dominic said was his favorite.

We talked while we drank strawberry and vanilla milkshakes, talked while we ate hamburgers and fries, talked while we ate ice cream melting over pecan brownies. We talked all the way to my street.

But as we walked toward my house, words suddenly evaporated. I was too nervous to think about whether he was nervous or bored or expectant. I didn't know what to do. Should I invite him in? He knew my parents weren't home. We'd had a great day and I didn't want it to end…but somehow it felt like it already had.

What would he think if he asked to come in and I said no?

How would I feel if he didn't ask?

We got to my driveway, the silence pressing in on me, making it hard to breathe. The earlier quiet had felt all right; now it felt wrong. We should be talking. I had taken a few steps up the driveway, focusing so hard on what I could possibly say that would sound light and natural that I didn't notice that Dominic had stopped at the sidewalk.

"Silke?"

I turned and looked at him in surprise.

"Thanks for settling your debt."

Arching an eyebrow at him, I asked, "Are we even now?"

He looked down and stubbed one of his toes into the curb a few times. "I think I may be in your debt now."

"What?"

"I...I had fun. A lot. I almost forgot.... It was...a great...fun day."

"Thanks, I think." I was confused. He was saying he had fun, but he sounded depressed. And he wasn't talking like him. He was hesitant, bashful even.

"Yeah, well," he looked down the street, squinting into the sunset. "I gotta go now."

"Oh," was all I could think to say.

I watched him slouch down the street and turn the corner. Then I let myself into my empty house and closed the door, not sure why the relief I should be feeling felt so much like disappointment.

Now I was listening as Bridget's phone went straight to voice mail.

"Hey, Bridget, it's Silke. Um, I should have talked to you earlier, but rumor has it that I'm staying at your house this weekend, and I'd really like it if you would, um, confirm that rumor if necessary. Call me as soon as you get home and I'll tell you everything."

I hung up, feeling like I had done too little too late. Mom was going to kill me and planning my own funeral now was probably my best use of time.

Suddenly I heard a strange squeaking noise. I walked around

the kitchen, listening intently, and determined that it wasn't coming from the fridge, dish washer, or the coffee maker. As I walked out into the hallway, though, the noise stopped.

I stood still for a few moments, waiting, but the noise didn't start again. So I went to the living room and turned on the TV. Might as well spend my last few hours of free living breaking more rules.

But there wasn't anything good on TV. I clicked it off and stood up — then froze. There was that noise again.

It was a noise that I felt I should recognize, but I didn't. The noise stopped. I started down the hall, walking past my room and Grete's room and the bathroom. I stopped just outside my parent's room. I wasn't allowed to go in their room without permission. I hesitated on the threshold, but the house was silent. Instead of going in, I went to my room.

As I turned on my computer, the noise started again.

"Enough already!" I yelled.

And the noise stopped.

"Arrgh!"

And the noise started again. I pushed back from my desk and ran to the hall. It was coming from Grete's room. I charged in, so irritated and scared at the same time that I didn't stop to think about what I was doing.

The noise stopped.

I turned a slow circle in the purple room, looking for the source. And then I saw the red eyes staring back at me.

The red, beady, rodent eyes.

Melvin.

I'd forgotten to take Melvin to Mrs. Childers last night. He still had food and water in his cage, though, so I didn't think he wasn't any worse for the neglect.

Melvin twitched his whiskered nose at me and began running in his squeaky wheel.

I picked up his cage and carried it back to the kitchen. Grabbing the Pioneer elementary school directory, I reached for my phone just as it rang.

Bridget lit up the screen. "Oh, thank you thank you thank you!" I said, flipping open the phone. "Thank you!"

"Where are you?" she demanded.

"At my house."

"At your house?"

"Yes."

"You're hiding at your house?"

"Yes, I mean, no. Well, yeah, sort of, I guess."

"Silke, what is going on?"

"I'm supposed to be staying at Alexi's—"

"—but she's sick, so you're not," Bridget interrupted. "Yeah, yeah, I know that. But why are you lying about staying with me?"

"I'm just staying at my house."

"Are you having a party?" she whispered excitedly.

"No!" I could barely handle the stress of what was going to happen when Mom found out I had lied to her; trying to throw a party would probably kill me.

"No?" Bridget sounded both disbelieving and disappointed.

"No," I said clearly. "But can you remember that I stayed at your house this weekend?"

"Sure. We watched movies, made cookies, and did some games. We had a blast," she finished flatly.

"Thanks," I said. "I owe you."

"Yeah. Remember that."

"I will." It struck me that lately I was giving out blank IOUs to people I didn't know very well.

"I expect a full report on Monday."

"You bet," I said, trying to put as much enthusiasm into my voice as I could. "See you then."

I took a few minutes, trying to settle down. It wasn't working very well, so I gave up and called Mrs. Childers. She offered to come get Melvin.

"Could you meet me at your house in about ten minutes?" she asked.

"Um, actually, we were just going out for ice cream," I said, surprised at how easily the thought came. Apparently lying was an easy habit to get into. "I'll bring him over on the way."

"Are you sure?"

"Yeah," I said. I didn't want to stay in the house. It was empty. And making me miserable.

CHAPTER NINE

So that was how I ended up walking down the street on Saturday night with a rat under my arm. Of all the ways I had envisioned spending my weekend, this was not it.

It was, however, kind of pleasant. It was almost dusk with a hint of pink still hovering along the horizon, and I had put on a light jacket before leaving the house. There were kids at the playground as I walked by. Their laughter drifted through the air and they were spinning the merry-go-round a lot faster than Dominic and I had.

I rang the bell at the Childers, and the door practically popped open the next second. Grete and Jilly had been waiting for me.

"Melvin!" they screeched together, yanking his cage out of my hands.

"Careful!" Mrs. Childers scolded from in the living room as they went pelting past her. "Hi, Silke. How are you?"

"Fine," I said. "How's Grete been?"

"Oh," she waved her hand, "She's a seven-year-old girl on her first sleepover. Excited, silly, and—" squealing came from down the hall where the girls had disappeared, "—loud."

I grinned. "Sounds like they're having fun."

"That's the point of a sleepover," Mrs. Childers said with a laugh.

I wondered if Grete would ever know how lucky she was to have her first sleepover at the Childers, instead of having a friend spend the night at our house. Mom insisted on inside voices at all times. Rules were rules, even if a friend was sleeping over.

"I've gotta go," I said, "Bridget's going to meet me at my house."

"I thought you were staying with the Amermans," Mrs. Childers said.

"Alexi had her appendix taken out on Friday," I explained. It was better to be completely truthful when I could. After all, it would be common knowledge that Alexi had surgery. "So I'm staying with Bridget Ulbricht instead."

"I don't know the name," Mrs. Childers said. "Is Bridget a ninth grader too?"

I nodded.

"Why is she meeting you at your house?"

"I need to pick a couple of things up." I smiled weakly. "Forgot my toothbrush."

"Ah," she said in an understanding tone.

"I've got to go," I said again.

"Of course," she said.

I almost called Grete to say good-bye, but I heard her high-pitched giggle and thought better of it. She was having fun. Let her be.

Walking home wasn't quite as nice. The temperature was dropping rapidly, and even though I zipped up my jacket, it was still chilly. It was full dark now, and the playground was empty.

As I turned onto my street, I realized that I should have left a light or two on in my house. It looked dark and desolate, the only house on the block that didn't have a single light on.

I stopped, uncertain. I needed to go home, I didn't have anywhere else to go, but I didn't want to go home.

A car drove by and honked right when it was next to me, scaring the crud out of me. Home looked better again.

Still, as I hurried down the street, I flipped open my cell phone. I hit speed dial two, and Alexi answered just as I turned up my driveway.

"I'm not talking to you," she said.

"I'm sorry," I said immediately. "I was a bad friend."

"Lousy."

"Awful," I agreed, unlocking the front door. "And I owe

you." Another blank IOU, but at least to someone I knew would never ask me to do anything stupid or risky.

"Humph."

"How are you feeling?" I locked the door behind me and then pulled on it twice before going farther into the house.

"Better, I guess. I'm really sore, but at least I'm not puking my guts out anymore."

"That's good."

"But then my supposed best friend goes and bails on everyone—"

"I didn't bail!"

"Do you know how freaked I was when I called Bridget and she had no idea what I was talking about? We called your house and you weren't there, either. We had no idea where you were! I almost told my mom!"

"I'm sorry, Alexi," I said as I turned on the living room and kitchen lights, and moved down the hall, turning on every light switch. "I really am. But I'm really, really glad you didn't tell your mom."

"Well, thank Bridget for that," she grumbled. "I was ready to tell Mom, but Bridget convinced me to wait a couple of hours. She said you were probably out with someone or at a party or something. I said you wouldn't do anything like that. I thought I knew you better."

"You do!" I protested. "I didn't go out for a party or anything. I just had a quiet evening at home."

"Humph."

"Look, Alexi, all I did was watch movies and order a pizza last night. Oh, and I went on Facebook too. You can check—I left you a get better bouquet and a new starfish for your reef." The house was well lit now, and I was methodically going room-to-room, tugging on windows to check the locks.

"I know. I got them this morning."

"Then—"

"Where were you *today*?" she interrupted. "When I called this morning and this afternoon, where were you?"

"I went out," I hedged. "Took a walk, had lunch, stopped at the playground...." I was being mostly truthful, but it was hard. I had been so ready to tell Alexi everything about today, so ready to hear her opinions about all of what Dominic did or didn't say, but suddenly I didn't want to tell her about him. I wanted to keep the day and him to myself. Without a doubt, she wouldn't understand.

"So why didn't you answer your phone?"

"I accidentally turned it off," I said honestly.

"And where are you now?"

"At home," I said.

"Hang on a sec."

I finished the last two windows in the kitchen. I looked at the door leading to the garage. Just as I took a step toward it, the house phone rang.

I grabbed the phone before I realized I should have checked caller ID first; I wasn't supposed to be home.

"Hello?" My voice quavered.

"Good," Alexi's cheerful voice said. "Just checking."

"Alexi!" but she had already hung up.

"Okay, I'm back," she said into her cell phone.

"What was that for?"

"I told you, just checking."

"You don't trust me?"

"Right now? No. You're not being yourself."

I squirmed on the inside. Alexi and I had been best friends since second grade, and I always loved that she seemed to know what I was thinking and feeling before I did. Now, though, I resented her empathy. "Alexi—"

"Do you know what your mother will do to you?" she demanded. "Do you know what she'll do to *me*?"

"She won't do anything to you," I said tiredly. When we were in third grade, Mom had yelled at Alexi for picking one of her flowers in the garden. Alexi had been terrified of her ever since.

"How can you say that? She won't let you come over here

ever again," Alexi said. "She'll cut us off."

"Just to punish me," I said.

"And you don't think it will affect me?" Alexi demanded.

"Okay, okay, I'm sorry," I said again. She had been my best friend for so long, and I always counted on her to help me do the right thing. But suddenly I felt like she was holding me back. "I'll make sure I don't get caught, okay. That was kind of my plan anyway, but if I have to worry about upsetting you, too, then I'll be extra careful."

"You'd better be."

"Have you talked to Adrian?" I asked, looking for a new topic.

It worked. Alexi launched into full detail about his calls (five), his Facebook message (complete with a virtual balloon bouquet), and was getting ready to read me the third e-mail he had sent her when I heard a voice in the background.

"I gotta go," Alexi said, "Mom wants me to rest."

"Okay," I said. "I'll call you tomorrow."

"You're not going anywhere, right?" she asked in a low voice.

"No, I'm staying right here."

"Do I have to call and check on you?"

"Alexi!"

"Okay. Talk to you tomorrow."

After I got off the phone with Alexi, I went around the house again, turning off all the lights. I settled in at the computer, but then I heard a thump from somewhere. So I got up and went back around, turning them on again. While I was in the kitchen, I opened the door to the garage, making sure it was empty. I locked the door between the house and the garage, even though it was something we didn't usually do.

The door going down to the basement didn't have a lock. I thought about walking down to make sure the basement was empty too, but I couldn't summon the courage. Instead, I wedged a chair under the doorknob as best as I could. I wasn't sure it would stop anybody from coming in through the basement (if they were already there), but I figured I would hear the commotion if someone tried to get out.

Back at the house computer, I sent Alexi an email and IM'd with Bridget and Daisy for a couple of minutes. But I didn't like sitting with my back to the office door. I signed off, and went to the kitchen, looking for dinner.

Nothing looked good in the fridge. I got a glass of lemonade. I made a prediction that Alexi would call to check on me at nine, but there wasn't anyone around to bet with.

For some reason, it suddenly occurred to me that I hadn't gotten the mail yesterday or today. I hurried out to the mailbox, and I actually ran back to the house. It didn't look as freaky with all the lights on, but I was having a hard time shaking the spooks.

Back in the kitchen, I flipped through the mail just because it was something to do. There was an envelope of advertisements, the kind that Mom always threw away without even looking at it, and I flipped through that as well.

A menu for Fang's Fortune House, our local Chinese restaurant, caught my eye. That sounded good. There was a 20% coupon on the bottom, too.

Before I really thought about it, I picked up the phone and ordered cashew chicken and fried rice.

"Twenty dollar minimum for delivery," the person at the restaurant said, sounding irritated.

"Oh." My order was eighty-three cents short, of course. "Um," I scanned the menu, looking for something good.

"Beef skewers? Egg rolls? Wonton soup?"

"Skewers," I said quickly.

"Anything to drink?"

I thought about getting a soda instead of the skewers, but decided, "No thanks."

"Total is twenty-three forty-five."

"With the coupon?"

"With the coupon. Be there in about twenty minutes."

"Thank you," I said, but they had already hung up.

I got a plate, fork, and large glass of water, and took it to the living room. I had just settled in the corner of the couch when the doorbell rang.

"That was fast," I was saying as I opened the front door.

"Didn't know you were timing me," Dominic said.

I wanted to snap at him for showing up again, but he was holding two Mongo Mugs. "Getting enough caffeine?" I asked.

"They were buy one-get one, and I didn't want it to go to waste." He grinned. "You strike me as a Cherry Coke kinda girl."

"Oh really?"

"Or you could have mine, if you'd rather."

"And what's that?"

"Half RedBull, half Mountain Dew, and a splash of Raspberry Tea."

"Turns out I *am* a Cherry Coke kind of girl," I said.

"Thought so." He handed me the plastic cup.

A horn honked, and he jumped.

"Expecting someone?" He asked as a car pulled in the driveway.

"Um-hmmm," I said.

The delivery guy sort of sprang out of his car and trotted up to the front porch. "Twenty-three forty-five," he read off the receipt.

I handed him the cash and he just took it and headed back to the car without counting.

"Guess I'll get out of your way," Dominic said.

"You don't have to go."

"But I haven't been invited to stay."

"You weren't invited to come over, either, and that didn't stop you," I said tartly.

A strange look crossed his face. It almost looked like sorrow.

"Have you eaten?" I asked.

"No."

"Come on in."

When he didn't move right away, I added, "Please?"

For a second I thought he was going to refuse. I clamped my lips together to prevent asking again. I wasn't going to beg.

"You sure you want me inside?" he asked, sounding oddly vulnerable.

"Dinner's getting cold," I said.

He smiled, and I wondered how I ever could have thought he looked dangerous. He was gorgeous.

*   *   *

I woke up with a start. Something was wrong. Very, very wrong.

Sunlight was streaming in through the living room windows; I'd forgotten to close the drapes before falling asleep on the couch again. I'd also forgotten to turn the TV off, and some evangelist was pounding his fist on an altar, which may have been what woke me up.

I rolled on my side, reaching for the remote on the coffee table. The TV snapped off just as the preacher said, "All sinners will repent and cry before our Lord!"

"Whatever," a voice mumbled below me.

I very nearly fell off the couch onto Dominic, who was stretched out on the floor between the couch and table, tucked in under Grete's Pretty Pony comforter. He shifted under the comforter, rolling on his side, and muttering something else that trailed off into a partial snore.

I'd forgotten to kick Dominic out.

He'd spent the night with me.

Okay, not that way, but who would believe me?

I took a breath. Scratch that. Who would believe *him*? No one would ever believe I let him spend the night.

And why exactly had I?

We'd eaten dinner and watched TV. Alexi did call to check on me, at 8:45. It was the only time that Dominic really shut up, but that may have been because I had my hand over his mouth. After that, TV got boring. I suggested playing

Monopoly, but when he saw Chutes and Ladders in the closet, we had to play that first.

Then we played Trouble, Candy Land, and Boggle. We never did get around to Monopoly. We made popcorn and melted cheese on crackers around midnight, and then found a good movie on TV. That's all I remember. I must have fallen asleep. Why hadn't he left? Maybe he had fallen asleep first, I thought. I really couldn't be sure I had fallen asleep before he did.

I looked at the clock. It was quarter past eight. If I kicked him out now, and a neighbor saw, it would look like he spent the night. If I waited till later, it could look like he had come over this morning.

"Breathe, Silke," he said below me, and I jumped. "No one's gonna find out."

"How did you know what I was thinking?"

"You looked terrified," he said flatly. "You were either worried about getting caught or you realized that you are absolutely in love with me. Scratch that," he said as he sat up, "Now I know the only thing that scares you more than the idea of being caught with me in the house is the thought of being in love with me."

"That's not true!" I exclaimed, pulling the afghan closer around me.

He stopped in mid stretch. "It's not?"

"I....I'm terrified of being in love with anybody," I said, while inside I was kicking myself. *Lame, lame, stupid, and more lame. So not smooth.*

"See?" he said, resuming his stretch. "I knew you were smart. Love is for idiots."

"You think so?"

"You don't?"

"I don't know. Never really thought about it."

"Then why are you afraid of being in love with anyone?"

I shrugged. I didn't have a good answer. And the conversation was making me even more uncomfortable than the fact that he had spent the night on the living room floor.

"Is it okay if I reheat the rest of that chicken?"

"For breakfast?"

"Well, it's a little early for lunch."

"You've got a point," I said.

Forty minutes later, we were putting the dishes away and it felt totally natural.

"That was the best omelet I've ever had," I told him. "I would have never thought of putting the chicken in it."

He grinned. "The cashews made it kinda different."

"Tasty!"

"So what are we doing today?" He asked.

"Um—" but I didn't get any further because my cell phone rang. My heart started thumping—it was Bridget. She was calling to say I was busted, I just knew it. "Hello?"

"We're going to the mall. Want a ride?"

"I don't—"

"You're supposed to be spending the weekend with me, remember?"

"But I—"

"I'm sick of being home, okay? And you owe me."

"What time?" I caved.

"Eleven."

"I'll meet you there."

"At the food court," she instructed.

"Okay."

"See you there!"

"Bye," I said, but she was already gone.

"Sounds like plans have been made." Dominic said with a strange expression on his face.

"Bridget wants me to meet her at the mall," I said, "and since she's covering for me this weekend—"

"You'd better go," he said with a small shrug.

"Want to come?" I asked, half-hoping he'd say no.

"Nah. The mall's not really my scene."

Surprisingly, I felt more disappointed than relieved. "I saw you at the mall before," I pointed out.

"I was running an errand."

"And you don't have any more to run?"

"Not at the mall."

"Oh."

He looked at the oven clock. "Just past nine," he said. "Is it too early to leave?"

"Could you wait until ten?" I asked, trying not to sound too pitiful.

"On one condition."

"What's that?"

"A rematch."

"A rematch?" I asked nervously, because he had a devilish grin.

"I know I can beat you at Chutes and Ladders this time."

"Dream on," I said, right before I bolted to the living room. He was barely a step behind me.

CHAPTER TEN

I was so bored at the mall. Bridget dragged me around from store to store, examining sweaters, shoes, and earrings, and made me hang out in front of the Lickin' Chicken to see if Adrian was working again. It was everything I usually lived for, but now it seemed pointless and stupid. Did I really care whether the blue in one sweater was a better match for my skin tone than the other one?

At first, I tried to act like I cared, but in less than an hour I could hear myself getting snippy with her and I couldn't seem to stop. After two hours I didn't try. When Bridgett finally said she was going home, I finally smiled.

I walked home instead of taking the bus, trying to figure out why I had been so out of it.

The only one I wanted to talk to was Dominic. He didn't seem to have any expectations of me. He didn't think I should be a goody-goody or a troublemaker or anybody but who I was—which was strange, because I was still trying to figure out who I was. But he was so hard to read. I never knew what he was going to do next, and it unnerved me a little bit.

I was beginning to wish the weekend had never happened. How could the magic hat screw me up so much?

My phone rang. I was tempted to ignore it. I didn't know what I'd say to anyone. But it was Dominic's name on my screen and I smiled. I desperately needed to hear a friendly voice.

"Yo Silke! Where you at? You done at the mall yet?"

In less than forty-eight hours, his voice had gone from creepy to soothing, and, even better, I had nothing to hide from him. "Yeah, I'm on my way home."

"Where are you?"

"On my way—"

He sighed. "*Where* are you? Have you passed twenty-fourth yet?"

"No. Why?"

"I'll meet you at the corner of twenty-fourth and Broadway."

"Why?"

"Try to do something spontaneous for once, without analyzing it."

"How's this for spontaneous?" I hung up.

My phone rang again.

"Just like that. See you in five."

And he was gone, before I could tell him that I hadn't agreed to meet him. But I would. I didn't know why, but I had to go meet him. And somehow, he knew it.

He was walking toward me on twenty-fourth, a couple blocks before I got to Broadway. I started smiling as soon as I saw him. I really couldn't help it. I told myself it was because the wind was blowing his hair all over, making him look like an overgrown rainbow Troll.

"You walk slow!" he bellowed when we were still practically a soccer field apart.

"You didn't say it was an emergency!" I yelled back.

"Life's an emergency!"

"Whatever." It was actually taking effort not to speed up. I concentrated on my steps, both shortening and slowing each of them.

"Now you're just being difficult," he said when we were close enough not to shout.

"You would know."

"How were the mall rats?"

"Diseased," I said, thinking of Bridget.

Dominic's eyebrows went up, but he didn't say anything. Instead, he did an about-face as I drew even with him, and began walking with steps perfectly matched to mine.

"Am I interrupting exciting plans for this afternoon?"

"Nope."

"Would you like some exciting plans?"

"That depends on what you have in mind."

"Ah, look at you, letting go with the flow!" And he took my hand.

Before this weekend, I had never held hands with a guy. But holding hands with Dominic already felt very natural.

"So you're not even going to ask?"

"Ask what?"

"Where we're going? What we're doing?"

"Nope," I said with a smile, "I'm just going with the flow."

He put his free hand over his heart and staggered two steps. "Wow. Just when I thought I knew you."

"No one really knows me," I said, and in my head a strange little voice said, *And that includes me, too.*

We hung a right on Broadway, heading toward the old part of the city. It used to be upscale, like back when my parents were kids. They had been trying to revitalize it for a couple of years, but from what I could tell, it hadn't made much progress.

It was a beautiful fall afternoon, and I felt like we could walk forever. I was disappointed when Dominic let go of my hand and fished keys out of his pocket.

"What's this?" He was unlocking a door, but instead of an apartment or townhouse front, it was a store. My peaceful mood popped like a bubble, and I felt a wave of fear wash over me. "What are you doing?" I couldn't stop the panicky screech that my voice became. I couldn't think of any good reason why he'd have a key to a beauty shop.

He looked over his shoulder at me. "What's wrong?"

"You're not here to tag it are you? Or...or rob it?"

Shaking his head, he pushed the door open. "Man, you stick the knife right between my shoulder blades when I'm least expecting it. Rob a store? Me? Not to mention the fact that I have a key!"

Meanwhile, he had flipped the light switch, and the florescent bulbs flickered to life, illuminating a small but clean beauty shop. It had four stations, and of those, only three of them had stuff on the counter.

"Have a seat," Dominic said, gesturing to the chair in front of the abandoned station. He tossed the keys on the counter in front of me, and disappeared in the back, making the hanging beads clatter.

I sat and immediately used my foot to spin the chair.

"What are we doing here?" I asked again, raising my voice so he could hear me in the back.

"Needen a tush uff."

"What?"

Dominic parted the beads, carrying several things in his arms and holding something between his teeth. He dropped all of it on the counter; a clattering mess of combs, pins, scissors, a plastic tub, paint brush, two plastic cups, and a couple of tubes. "Needed a touch up," he said, moving the things around.

"You do your own hair?"

"Why do you sound surprised?"

"I just…it looks…it seemed….How do you do it in the back?"

"Multiple mirrors," he said, pulling two out of the tub. He suctioned one of them to the big mirror at a ninety-degree angle.

I watched him in silence for a few minutes, while Dominic set everything up, disappearing into the back room twice, coming back with towels and plastic wrap, broom and dust pan.

"Is this where you work?"

"Nah," he said.

"But you know what you're doing."

He shrugged.

"Could you tell me what you're doing?"

"I did. Touch-ups."

"Which color?"

He stopped cold and stared at me. Just when I started to squirm because I thought I had insulted him, he grinned.

"Silke, you're so cool. Anyone else would be suggesting that I change to one color or even cut all the color off, but you just want to know which color I'm touching up."

I was so glad I hadn't suggested he try a nice auburn this time. "So which color?" I pressed.

"Actually, I'm not so much touching-up as tipping off."

"Tipping off?"

He snipped the top off one of the tubes and squeezed the content into one of the cups. As he did the same with the second tube, he said, "I'm just going to do the tips of my hair."

"Which brings us back to the all important question: which color?"

"Silver."

I blinked. "Silver?" Of all the colors on his head, that wasn't one of them. So it made sense, then, that he would want to add it.

"Well, I'm aiming for silver. It'll probably just go white, though."

He began parting his hair in sections. Watching him, I realized how exact each line was. There were eight colors on his head, and each color had four sections, two on each side. When he was done, he had 32 little ponytails tied off.

"Why divide into so many colors?"

"I like variety."

"Sincerely."

"I am sincere. I like options and choices."

"But aren't you tipping all of the colors white? Why do you have to do them separately?"

"So that they'll all have the same quarter inch of white," he said, using the paintbrush to apply the mixture to the tip of a red ponytail.

"Oh." I watched as he painted a green and then a blue ponytail. "Want help?"

He stopped, brush in mid air. "Really?"

Standing up, I held out my hand.

"I don't know," he said, "You might slip and paint more

than a quarter inch."

"I'll be very careful."

Dominic started to hand me the brush, but then he pulled back. "Would you let me do your hair?"

I froze. I wanted to scream, 'Not even if hell froze over!' but I was afraid that might offend him.

He seemed to know what I was thinking. "It'd be great if you helped," he said, handing me the brush, "especially in the back."

"I'll be very careful," I repeated as he took the chair I had just vacated.

"I trust you."

I tipped three ponytails. He didn't say anything, so I looked up into the mirror. His eyes were closed. He wasn't even watching. I smiled, and finished tipping the rest of his ponytails, each one only a quarter of an inch.

*   *   *

After he let it set and then rinsed it out and dried it, he surveyed it critically, using four different mirrors to check from every angle.

"Silke," he said finally, "You do fine work."

I felt absurdly pleased and embarrassed at the same time. "It looks fantastic," I said, trying to cover up my embarrassment.

He stopped combing his hair. "You think so?"

I nodded. It did. I would have never thought something like that could look so cool, but it did. The ring of white under all the colors... "It looks like a halo that slipped down to your neck," I said.

He cocked his head to one side and then the other, studying his reflection. Then he laughed. "That's me. Being strangled by a halo!"

I helped him clean up the rest of his supplies.

In a matter of minutes, we were out on the street again. It was dusky, and the air smelled of an impending rain. I was in the middle of a stretch, smiling up at the sky, when an angry voice suddenly yelled, "What the hell do you think you're doing?"

I went from arms wide stretched and stomach arching out to arms wrapped around my middle, hunched over to protect myself.

Dominic, however, was turning from locking the door with a huge grin on his face. "Ivy! Good to see you!"

Ivy did not seem too happy to see Dominic. She was glaring at him so fiercely I could almost feel the air around us dropping in temperature. Her hair was a vibrant red that clearly wasn't natural, but she seemed to have the temper associated with red heads.

"You—"

"Remembered to clean up this time," Dominic said.

"You are—"

"Coming in to help you tomorrow."

"You—" Ivy kept trying, but she wasn't shouting or glaring any more.

"I'm sorry that I didn't call," Dominic said softly.

A strange look crossed her face. "You promised," she said.

"I'm sorry."

They looked at each other for a long moment. I wanted to evaporate and not leave a trace.

"I've been so worried."

"I know," Dominic said. "But you don't need to be."

"How's—"

"Fine," Dominic snapped curtly, his gentle tone completely gone. "It's all good."

"Dominic—"

"I've got to walk Silke home," he said, back to his normal voice.

"Oh, oh, I'm sorry," Ivy said, turning to me. "I didn't mean—"

"It's all right," I said. I had no idea what was going on. Ivy seemed to understand.

"Dominic's supposed to call when he's at the store. Mr. McKinney called to say a couple of kids were screwing around inside."

"You should've known it was me," Dominic said.

"If it was just one kid, then sure," Ivy smiled at me in a mischievous way. "You've never brought a friend before."

"Well, I've got to get my new friend home now."

"I'm Aunt Ivy," she said, now ignoring Dominic and focusing on me. "And you're Silke?"

"Yes," I said, accepting her handshake.

"Do you have classes with him?"

"Western Civ."

"Is he doing all right? Is he going to school regularly? Staying out of trouble?"

"Um—" I shot a look at Dominic.

"We're leaving," he said, stepping forward and taking my arm. He looped his elbow with mine, the way guys used to escort girls around a long, long time ago.

"It was really nice meeting you, Silke. I hope to see you again soon. Bye!" she called after us. Dominic wasn't gripping my arm, but he was undoubtedly in control of where we were going.

"So that's your aunt," I said as we moved down the street.

Dominic snorted. "She's not my aunt."

"But—"

"She's my mom's best friend from high school. She likes to pretend she's my aunt."

"And that's her shop?"

"Only if she's my aunt."

"What?"

"It's my mom's place."

"Oh. Then—"

"Want to go get dinner?"

"Um—"

"This way," and he turned me toward Jefferson Avenue.

The river walk off Jefferson was bursting with people. I

didn't know it'd be so crowded on a Sunday night. Dominic began a running commentary on all the people we saw, like he had done at Wal-Mart. He was funny, but not nearly as funny as he had been before. He was trying too hard.

Clearly he didn't want to talk about his 'Aunt Ivy' and the beauty shop, and he was afraid I was going to dig for information. And on any other day, I probably would have. But I was tired of everything being a fight. I enjoyed our time in the beauty shop, and I wanted to enjoy dinner too.

I wanted to let everything go.

It was my last night without stress and pressure to do everything right. I was going to make the most of it.

CHAPTER ELEVEN

Dinner was great. We waited nearly an hour to get seated, but Dominic assured me that the food was worth the wait and he was right. The garlic bread and salad was more than enough to fill me up, but the tortellini Alfredo a la Riccia practically melted in my mouth.

I argued when Dominic paid the bill, but only half heartedly; I had spent way too much money this weekend and was going to have a hard time explaining to my mother where all my cash had gone.

We talked about everything except his 'Aunt Ivy' it seemed. He told me so many fascinating things about himself that I kept getting sidetracked.

I was stunned to find out that he was a skater—not a skate boarder, but a figure skater. Pairs.

"Who's your partner?" I asked, once I recovered from choking on my soda.

"Don't have one anymore," he said, tearing off another piece of garlic bread. "I quit."

"Who was your partner?"

"You wouldn't know her."

And already I knew him well enough to know that he didn't want to talk about that, either.

He told me almost everything else, though. His parents divorced when he was four, which didn't bother him, but his dad had remarried last year, which did. His new stepmother was young and very strict (though I was sure not as strict as mine), and expecting Dominic's half-sister any day now. He had begun skating at age three, was on a hockey team until he was seven. That's when he decided to switch to figure skating, because he got sick of spending half of his games in the penalty box.

He told me he had been put ahead a year in second grade, and that he had wet his bed until he was nine. He told me that he had gone to a private junior high, and had been on academic scholarship. Dolphins were his favorite animals, but he was afraid of the water ("Unless it's frozen," he said with a grin.) He was an avid Redwings fan, and was mad that our high school didn't have a fencing team.

He was completely open about almost everything, and had me completely confused. I couldn't make sense of him. But he seemed to know everything about me, even ordering a lemon cream pie for dessert, without me telling him that I didn't like chocolate very much.

It was like he was inside my head.

I asked him to come back to my house with me.

"I don't think so," he said, shaking his head.

"Come on, it's Sunday night. We could watch a movie." I didn't want to admit that I was a little afraid of going home alone.

"Dinner and a movie? That sounds suspiciously like a date," he said with a grin, "I'm still worried you're going to fall in love with me."

"Ha, ha!" I said, though my tummy did roll a little bit. He hadn't shown any interest in me *that way* at all. "You know I just need to have you around in case Mrs. Amerman calls and wants to talk to Mr. Ulbricht again."

"Of course! Why didn't you just say so?" He looked so relieved, I felt hurt. "How about I meet you there in an hour or two?"

"What, you don't want me to know where you live?"

"No."

The answer was so abrupt and unexpected, it was like he had slapped me. I turned away so he wouldn't see the tears welling in my eyes.

"Then just forget it," I snapped, trying to match his abruptness. "Go home."

He reached for my hand and I tried to snatch it away. I wasn't strong enough.

"Silke."

I stood there, glaring away from him, feeling the stupid tears spill over and down my cheeks.

"Silke," he said again in that deep, deep voice that was silkiness itself. "It's not like that."

I refused to look at him. I tried to jerk my hand away. The third time I pulled, he let go, and I staggered forward two steps.

"Come on," he sighed. "Let's go."

We walked back to Broadway, and then caught the bus. It was dark now. If I had been alone, I would have been relieved to be on the bus. With him, I wished we were walking home slowly and talking, making the night last even longer.

Instead, we weren't talking at all and the bus barreled toward home much too fast.

The bus got to my stop and I stood up. Dominic didn't.

"Can I call you later tonight?" he asked, almost sounding meek.

"No," I said, wanting to be as abrupt and cruel as I felt he had been.

"Silke, I'm sorry."

"Whatever." I got off the bus and started walking toward my house without looking back. Very often.

Home seemed so strange without him in it. I thought about calling Alexi and asking if I could come spend the night at her house. But if I went to Alexi's, her mom would know something had happened. And even if I called Alexi, she would know something was wrong, just from my voice. I would have to tell her everything. It would make a bad night even worse.

I realized that I hadn't checked FB in more than twenty-four hours, which was something of a record for me. I wondered what had happened in my cyber reality.

My home page opened to show my friends' status:

Alexi Amerman (6:57): Hates everything!
Daisy Molina (6:58): forgot to bring home math homework!
Bridget Ulbricht (6:52): Just finished math and science.
Danny McCauley (6:45): sent you a smile! Send a smile
                back to Danny.
Emma Hawkins (6:31): see you all tomorrow, peeps!
Emma Hawkins (6:30): sent hugs to her friends. Send a hug
                back to Emma!
Daisy Molina (6:12): Tired of babysitting—but have $ for
                    next weekend! Who's up 4 the party?
Emma Hawkins (6:10): Where is every1?
Alexi Amerman (6:08): the stupid stitches itches!
        Emma Hawkins (6:09): cute!
        Alexi Amerman (6:09): doesn't feel cute.

I updated my status first:

Silke Reichard (7:04): a blue world through rose-colored
                glasses leaves one purple.

Alexi was on line, so I clicked on chat, and started typing. If
Alexi couldn't see my face or hear my voice, it would be easy
to act like everything was normal.

Silke Reichard (7:05):→ Alexi Amerman: Hi! How are you?

I waited for two minutes for her response, but then she
signed out of Facebook, without messaging me at all.
    Others had responded to my status, though.

Taylor Keeler (7:07): Yellow and blue make green!
Danny McCauley (7:07): what?

I smiled, but I wasn't in the mood to keep posting. I signed
off and shut down the computer. Did it really matter what was
going on in cyberspace?

I'd forgotten all about the math and science homework. I should do it.

I left the books in my backpack and headed to the kitchen. I wasn't really hungry, so I just walked around the kitchen and then went to the living room. I turned the TV on, flipped through eight or nine channels, and then turned it off again.

I didn't want to do anything but cry, and I didn't know why.

But I went to my room and cried anyway.

*   *   *

Apparently I hadn't realized how tired I was, because I dozed off. I jerked awake. It was almost nine-thirty. My days of freedom were nearly over. I was not going to end them wallowing in self-pity, crying on my bed.

So what was I going to do? First, I washed my face. Not really exciting, but I knew it would make me feel better. I studied my reflection. My eyes weren't too red or puffy. My face was just as pale as normal, and my ultra fine, blonde white hair was parted in a straight line down the middle and lay flat against my head, just as it normally did. Just as it had ever since I had hair.

My hair had always been long and straight and flat. Once a month, Mom trimmed Grete and my hair. Simple and efficient was the rule at our house. I had never had a real haircut, or perm, or even a real style. Mom didn't like change.

I skipped down to the kitchen, grabbed the scissors and ran back to the bathroom. Running with scissors in my hand and laughing—I felt the need to rebel pulsing through my very soul.

I wasn't laughing ten minutes later, though. Cutting in a straight line was not easy. I had only wanted a simple set of long bangs. Now, I was staring at my lopsided bangs that were almost up to my left eyebrow. I needed to even them out, but I was terrified that I would only succeed in making them shorter and more lopsided—the way I had the first two times I tried to even them out. I set the scissors down on the counter and forced myself to take a step back.

"Take a breath," I told myself out loud. "Take a break. Settle down. Grab a snack. Come back with a new view."

In the kitchen, nothing looked good or appetizing. I decided that making a batch of cookies would be a good way to relax, get a snack, and take my mind off the haircut all at once. It was late to start, but I didn't care. Cookies were what I wanted. I turned on the radio and set to work.

I was sliding the second cookie sheet into the oven when a knock came from the window above the kitchen sink.

Two nights ago, I would have screamed and either flung the cookie sheet across the room or burned my hand on the oven. Tonight, though, I only flinched. And smiled to myself as I closed the oven and set the timer. Then I grabbed the spatula.

He knocked again. I needed to give the first cookies a minute to cool before I slid them off the sheet anyway. So I turned and leaned against the counter.

Dominic was framed in the window. His face was pale and his hair was rumpled. I knew that he hadn't made his hair look like that on purpose; this time it wasn't a style. He looked almost forlorn.

He pointed to the sliding glass door.

I crossed my arms.

He held a piece of paper up to the window. It had a jagged edge, like it had been rapidly torn out of a spiral notebook. In big block green letters, it said SORRY.

I turned my back and began using the spatula to lift the cookies from the sheet to the cooling rack. Dominic knocked on the window again. I carefully moved all of the cookies to the cooling rack before turning around again.

Now the paper said SINCERELY. He flipped it over so it said SORRY again. He flipped it back and forth twice more.

I tried to stop the smile. I couldn't. He pointed at the sliding glass door again. I nodded.

"I'm sorry," he was saying as I pulled the door open.

"Sincerely," I said.

"Very sincerely seriously sorry," he said. I turned to move back to the oven, but he reached out and grabbed my arm. "What'd you do to your hair?"

I grimaced and pulled away. "Cut it," I muttered.

"Using what? A harvesting scythe?"

"Nice. An insult immediately following an apology. You must have been seriously sincere."

"Sorry," he said again. "It just...looks..."

"Horrid," I said, opening the oven to check on the cookies even though the timer said they had another eight minutes.

"Rough," he corrected. "It just looks a little rough, so if that's what you're going for, it looks great."

I didn't turn from the oven.

"But you're not really a rough person, if you ask me."

"I know," I groaned. "It's awful."

"No," he said, taking my shoulders and turning me around. He studied me critically and impersonally. "It just needs some smoothing."

"Smoothing?"

He took a lock of hair and lifted it from my shoulder. I got goosebumps. "Smoothing," he said again, "These blunt angles have got to go."

"Really? Go where?"

"Away," he said, taking his hands off my shoulders, leaving a slight chill. "Where are the scissors?"

"In the bathroom."

He took my hand, and started to walk out of the kitchen. I planted my feet. He turned and looked at me with a raised eyebrow. "Cookies," I said, pointing at the oven.

"With milk?" he asked. He sounded and looked like a kindergartener. A kindergartener with a freaky hairstyle, but still.

So we sat down and ate the cookies almost as fast as they came out of the oven. We finished the gallon of milk. He helped me rinse the dishes and put them in the dishwasher.

S.L. ROTTMAN

"Ready?"

"For what?" I asked.

He made snipping actions with his fingers.

"Oh," I said, reaching up and pulling on my bangs. I had almost forgotten about them.

"Let's go."

Excuses came bubbling up, but I forced them back down. I compressed my lips and nodded, afraid of allowing an excuse to escape.

He led the way back to the bathroom as if he had grown up in my house. He was so confident and comfortable. Dominic probably never second-guessed anything he did.

"Chair?"

"Hmm?" I asked, realizing that he had stopped and was staring at me.

"Do you have a chair to sit on?"

"Can't I just sit on the toilet?" I asked, blushing.

"Then I can't get to the back," he said.

"The back? Who said anything about the back?" I asked, but he was disappearing into my room. Moments later he was pushing my desk chair into the bathroom.

"All I want is straight and even bangs."

He grabbed a towel and put it around my shoulders, pushing me down into the chair. He walked behind me, pulling my hair out from under the towel and letting it fall lightly. He leaned forward so his face was over my left shoulder, and our eyes met in the mirror.

"Oh, no," he said softly by my ear.

"No?"

"You want much more than straight and even bangs."

"I do?"

"Yes."

"What do I want?"

"You want to trust me."

I stared at our faces in the mirror, my pale hair next to his rioting rainbow. My blue eyes were locked on his green ones.

Swallowing, I nodded and said, "I do."

"Sincerely?"

"Yes."

"Good."

He turned me around and picked up the scissors and comb. When he lifted the first section, I squeaked, "Dominic!"

"What?"

"Can't I watch?"

"I thought you trusted me."

"I do."

"Than *trust* me."

I took a deep breath.

"Ready?" He asked.

"Yes." And I was. I closed my eyes. I breathed easily. I let go.

CHAPTER TWELVE

"What?"

Dominic was staring at me, head tilted to one side. We were sitting in the living room, watching a late movie.

He had done an amazing job with my hair. My bangs were straight, but he hadn't stopped there. He had layered my hair, giving it more life than it ever had before. It framed my face now, instead of just laying against my cheeks. I couldn't wait to show Alexi. I felt like someone new. I felt glamorous and attractive.

But with Dominic staring at me, I felt odd. "What?" I demanded again.

"I think it's time."

"Time?"

"Yep. You're ready."

"Ready for what?"

He rolled off the couch instead of answering. "Let's go."

"Where?

"Come on, Silke. I thought you were past this. I thought you trusted me."

"Well, yeah, but—"

"Uh-uh," he said, wagging a finger back and forth in front of me, "No buts. Either you trust or you don't, there's no 'I trust you, but' or 'kind of' trust." He grabbed his jacket and pulled it on. "So what do you say?"

Three minutes later, we were walking down the dark street. I was dying to know where we were going, but I couldn't think of a good way to ask without implying that I didn't trust him.

"Race you!" he said suddenly.

"That's not fair," I objected, "I don't know where we're going."

"Bet you can figure it out!" And he took off.

I thought about not chasing him. For half a second.

At the end of the street, he had a ten-step lead on me, but then, suddenly, I knew where he was going, and I turned up the speed.

Charging into the elementary school playground, we were side-by-side. Our feet hit the gravel at the same time.

"I won!" he gasped.

"No way!"

"Did too!"

"Did not!"

"Fine!" He collapsed on the merry-go-round. "You won."

"Did not."

He looked at me in surprise. "What?"

"We tied," I said.

"Yeah," he said with a grin, "I guess we did." For several seconds we sat there, catching our breath. Then he stood up. "All right. Time to get to work!"

"Work?"

He reached down and grabbed my hand, pulling me up. "Work," he said, and then he reached into his coat pocket and pulled out two cylinders. I thought they looked familiar, but until he shook one and it rattled, I didn't recognize the spray paint.

"You're kidding." I stepped back from him. "Vandalism is not work. Nor is it cool."

"Hmm," he said, popping the lid off of one can while he slid the other one back into his pocket. "If you say so."

He took the can, and began spraying the merry-go-round. I was so mad, I turned around and took a few steps away, but the steady hiss of the spray paint didn't stop. I turned back around to see what he was doing.

Instead of doing wide, careless swoops, he was methodically spraying the bars, carefully coating them. He wasn't tagging them or damaging them; he was repainting them.

"What are you doing?"

"Painting."

I walked back over to him. He had finished the first bar and moved to the next one. He wasn't doing a perfect job—even in the dark I could see that he was spraying some on the bottom of the merry-go-round as well—but he was making sure the entire bar was covered.

As he moved on to the third bar, he said, "Are you going to just stand there? Or are you going to help?"

And that's how I ended up on the playground with a can of spray paint in my hand on Sunday night.

Dominic instructed, "Do every other panel under the bars. I'm not really sure that two cans will be enough for the whole thing."

"Have you done this often?"

"I've done it before," he said, but didn't elaborate.

It wasn't until I was painting the second panel that I figured out how to stay far enough away from the fumes to keep from choking, while still being close enough to apply the paint evenly.

"See, sometimes things that should be good are bad, and things that should be bad—"

"—are good," I finished for him.

"Exactly."

"But this is, like, community service."

"Is it? Is that what you're going to tell the cops?"

I dropped the can and spun around, heart thudding painfully in my chest, but the playground was still empty.

"Relax. Joking. But do you think they'd buy your 'community service' plea?"

"No," I said, and I was thinking about Alexi. She would be appalled. And Mom. She would say this was vandalism. No matter what the reason or the out come, Mom was unable to see anything good when rules were broken.

We ran out of paint before we had completely finished the merry-go-round, but only one of the floor panels and the center octagon were left untreated.

"I'll get another can tomorrow," Dominic rumbled as we crunched our way out of the gravel. "It should only take one more can to finish up."

"And when will you do that?"

"It will probably be a few days," he said, "since I have to do my good deeds under the cover of darkness."

We walked back to my house. While Dominic flopped on the couch and flipped through the channels, I raided the kitchen. I went for things we hardly used, hoping that Mom and Dad wouldn't notice them missing. I brought out some crackers and cheese, and two cans of diet soda.

I curled up in the corner of the couch. "What's on?"

"Nothing good," he said. He flipped through a couple more channels, and then turned the TV off. "What happened to you?"

"What do you mean?"

He propped his chin on his fist. "What made you call me last week?"

"Mr. Norton made us exchange numbers, remember?"

He shook his head. "Yeah, but you almost said no when I asked for your number. I was sure you'd never call me, even if you missed a whole week of school."

I looked down, surprised at how close he was to knowing my exact thoughts.

"So why'd you call?"

"Magic," I said.

"Huh?"

"I pulled your name from a magic hat."

"Silke, were you drinking something before I got here?"

I laughed, and then tried to explain the magic hats to him.

"So what kind of things are in these hats?"

I shrugged. "All sorts of stuff. 'Call a friend.' 'Go out to dinner.' 'Go to Vegas.'"

"Go to Vegas?"

"Well, that's for my parents," I said. "That's where they are right now."

"Cool! Can I see this hat?"

"Why?"

"I want to know where my pre-destined weekend with you came from."

"You're so odd!"

He grinned and stood up. "Come on," he said. "I want to see the magic hat."

I led him down the hall to my parents' bedroom, feeling very strange. It was almost worse than having Dominic spend the night. I stopped at the threshold. Dominic, of course, walked right in. He looked around.

"Where are they?"

Swallowing hard, I walked over to the closet and opened the door. Wordlessly, I pointed to the top shelf.

"Cool," he said, reaching up and grabbing the top hat. "A relic from the day, huh?"

"Yeah," I said.

Dominic handed it to me and then reached for the fedora. "And this one's yours?"

"Yep."

He took it to my parents' bed and sat down. "So what kinds of things are in here?"

"A trip to the movies, a day at a museum, a new pair of shoes..." I trailed off.

"What else?"

"I don't know."

"Let's look."

"What?"

"Let's see what you've got coming," he said as he pulled a piece of paper from the hat.

Even though I hated that hat, it surprised me how much it bothered me to see him reaching into it. I set the top hat on the edge of the bed and reached for the fedora. Dominic let me take it, because he was unfolding the paper.

"'Join a team,'" he read out loud. "What's that mean?"

"Just what it says." My heart sank as if I had read the note with my parents. Join a team? Why? When would I even have time?

"Should we throw it away?"

"What?" I tried to drag myself out of the terror of having to join a new group and focus on what he was saying.

"You don't look that thrilled," he said. "So why don't we just throw it away?"

"We can't do that."

"Why not?" He nodded toward the fedora. "Who's going to miss one slip of paper?"

"It'd be cheating."

"So?"

"What if I had thrown away the one that said to do something different?"

"What if you had done something else, like starting a rock band, instead of just calling someone new?" he countered. "It may have taken longer for you to warm up to me, but it would have happened anyway."

"Oh?" I found his arrogance annoying. "What makes you think that?"

"Because," he began as he stood up, "Dest—"

"Watch out!"

When he stood up, the mattress shifted and the top hat fell from the bed. We both grabbed for it and we both missed.

It bounced on the floor and dumped out most of the little pieces of paper, scattering them like confetti. Additional slips of paper fell with it, because I leaned forward with the fedora in my arms, dumping half of it.

Dominic sank to the floor and began scooping up paper right away. "I'm sorry, Silke," he said. "I didn't mean to."

"Wait!" I said as he shoved a handful into the top hat. "Stop!"

"What?"

"We have to make sure that they go in the right hat," I said.

"And how are we going to know that?"

"We won't on all of them," I said as I sat down next to him,

"But some of them will be obvious, like this one, 'Afternoon at the mall,' is mine."

"Blech. Give it to your parents."

I laughed and put it in the fedora.

"Damn, Silke, how many times do your parents need to go to Vegas?"

"What do you mean?"

"I mean all of these," he held up six pieces of paper, "Say 'Go to Vegas.'"

"What are you talking about?" But even as I said it, three slips of paper that had landed face up stared at me, all saying 'Go to Vegas.' If I hadn't been sitting, I would have fallen down. "I don't believe it."

My mind whirled. Dad had wanted to go to Vegas for years, and now he had gotten what he wanted. By rigging the hat. It was the only explanation that made sense, but I couldn't understand it either. Dad cheated? I couldn't believe it, but as I turned more paper slips over, the truth was in pieces in front of me.

Had he done it before? Had he done it to me? Last spring, less than two weeks after I had fallen off my bike, I drew a sheet that said 'Take an afternoon bike ride.' Had the hats always been rigged?

Some of the slips were turning up different. Go to a movie, have a sleepover, two extra hours of internet time, deep clean your room (which meant moving the furniture to vacuum under it as well as wiping down the walls and washing the windows), read a Civil War era book, go to the graphic art convention—those were all for me.

But the rest—I dumped the top hat out, shaking it violently before tossing it against the wall.

Dominic understood. He didn't say a word as I set slip after slip down on the floor. He sat next to me and helped, until finally there were eighty-four slips staring up at me, all saying 'Go to Vegas.'

I sat and stared at them. Dominic moved on to the fedora,

emptying it. All of those slips were different.

"Should we check Gert's?"

"Who?"

"Your sister?"

"Grete," I said absently, "No."

The clock in my parents' room ticked noisily in the silence—un-real, un-real, un-real—I heard over and over in my mind.

"Should we rig yours?" he rumbled.

"No." He didn't argue, just waited. Finally I swept up all the 'Go to Vegas' slips.

"Put those in the fedora," Dominic suggested. "I'll go with you."

I didn't answer as I retrieved the top hat and dumped the Vegas papers in. I replaced the hat on the closet shelf, and Dominic was right next to me, sliding the fedora on the shelf. We returned to the living room.

"Shall I find the beer?" Dominic asked as I flopped on the couch. "Or vodka?"

I didn't answer, just stared off in space.

"Do you want me to go home?"

I looked up and blinked. "Please don't."

"Okay. I'll be right back."

He left, and then I heard him rattling around in the kitchen.

I wondered what he was doing; part of me was afraid he was finding the alcohol, part of me was hoping he was. But I didn't care enough to get off the couch.

I felt like the world had been pulled out from under me.

Everything was according to rule. Everything was about doing it right. Everything was absolute.

Except everything was an absolute cheat.

"Here you go," Dominic said, and I had to laugh. He was carrying a tray, looking very professional. The tray held two steaming mugs, the last five cookies we hadn't been able to stuff down, and a small stack of napkins.

"What is that?"

"Hot chocolate."

"Hot chocolate? What'd you put in it?"

"Nothing. I couldn't find any marshmallows."

"You didn't put vodka or beer in it?"

He wrinkled his nose. "I wanted to make you feel better, not sick."

"Thanks," I said, wrapping my hands around the warm mug. "So what now?"

"Tell me a story."

"A story?"

"Yeah."

"Um. Once upon a time, a boy was born. He grew up. He died. The end."

"That's a sucky story."

He shrugged. "It's all stories," he said, "When you get down to it."

"Yeah, but—"

"Or it's a girl who's born, grows up, lives and dies. Life isn't sexist."

And it's not fair, either, because not all of them really live while they grow up, I thought to myself. I took a sip of cocoa and nibbled on a cookie. The house was supremely quiet, and I liked it. But I still wanted to know more about Dominic.

"Why didn't you want to come over tonight?"

"I'm here, aren't I?"

I looked into my mug of tea. "You didn't want to come over."

"If I didn't want to, I wouldn't be here," he said flatly.

"You changed your mind," I countered.

"I finished my task."

"What task?"

"Something I had to do."

"And I couldn't go with you?"

"It wasn't your type of place."

"And how do you know what type of place is mine?" I demanded.

He studied me for a moment and then smiled. "I don't, anymore."

"What?"

"You've changed," he said, shaking his head.

"You just met me."

"I know," he said, "That's what makes your change so surprising."

It was strange, how deeply entrenched he was in my mind. I *had* changed—I could feel it, though I didn't feel done yet. "So why couldn't I go with you?"

"Because I wasn't comfortable taking you. I wasn't trying to hurt you."

"I know."

"So will you let it go already?"

"Okay," I said. "Why'd you get suspended?"

"What?"

"Why'd you get suspended?"

"I didn't."

"The second day of school—"

"I wasn't suspended."

"You lied to me?"

He squirmed a little. "It was for a good reason."

"Really?" I asked skeptically. "Where were you?"

"Busy."

"Dominic…"

"Silke…." He whined back.

"Tell me. You don't keep secrets."

"I don't broadcast, either."

"So share."

"Later."

I opened my mouth but something about his expression made me snap my mouth shut instead.

"Mind if I turn the TV back on?"

"Go ahead," I said, tossing him the remote. "Knock yourself out."

"Want the last cookie?"

"It's all yours."

He grinned and snatched the last cookie, and then he hesitated. "Want half?"

I shook my head and he stuffed the entire thing in his mouth. Snuggled under the afghan, sipping cocoa and watching TV with the freaky guy from school, I felt warm and content, all the way through.

Because I realized it was time to stop letting rules ruin my life. Too much had been done by rules that didn't matter. It was time to take charge, but it was also time to leave a few things to chance.

CHAPTER THIRTEEN

"Silke! Silke, wake up!"

I burrowed further under the blanket.

"Silke, you're late for school!"

"Who cares?"

"You'd better!"

"I'm busy."

Dominic snorted. "You're sleeping, not busy."

I cracked one eye open. "I bet you slept when you were too busy to go to school."

"You'd lose."

"What time is it?"

"Almost eight."

"Okay," I said.

"Okay? You've already missed half of first hour!"

"Yep. There's no way I'd get there any earlier than second hour, but I'd probably miss that too. If I were going."

"You're not going?"

"Nope."

"Why not?"

That was a fair question. And I thought I had a fair answer. But I didn't want to tell him. "I'm gonna take a shower," I said, rolling off the couch and standing up.

Dominic was staring at my head.

I reached up. I could feel my new bangs sticking straight up. Before, the thought of standing in front of a boy without having my hair carefully styled would have sent me flying from a room. Today I couldn't care less.

"I need a shower too," Dominic said. "Mind if I use your parent's bathroom?"

"Um—" I thought about using my parents' bathroom myself,

and letting him use mine, but all my makeup and stuff was in there. "Sure," I said. I was going to have to clean the house anyway. Might as well clean out their bathroom too.

He took forever. By the time he came out of the bathroom, I had cleaned my bathroom and the kitchen, and vacuumed the living room. Today he had managed to part his hair so he had six ponytails sticking up, and each one showed a different color.

"So, do you still like your hair?"

"Yeah," I said. I had wanted to stare at myself in the bathroom, but made myself hurry so I wouldn't keep Dominic waiting, which, evidently, had been pointless.

He tilted his head again. "Hmmm."

"What?"

"It's good," he said, "But it could be better."

"How's that?"

"You need a splash of color. Maybe a little..." he tilted his head to the other side. "....ummm, a little lavender."

I laughed. "Yeah, right, like I'm going to dye my hair purple."

He shook his head. "You weren't listening. I said lavender."

"Same thing."

"No. Not at all. Especially when you're talking hair color."

"Not gonna happen."

"Okay," he said with a shrug. "So what *is* going to happen?"

I glanced at the clock. Mom and Dad would be home around one-thirty, if their flight arrived on time. I wasn't supposed to be home until after three.

"I should go to the grocery store. Mom's going to wonder who ate all the food this weekend."

"Good point. What else?"

"I just need to be gone until school gets out."

"Oh, snap!" he said suddenly. He grabbed his phone and pulled it out of his pocket. "My mom's name is Lori. I'm not feeling good today, okay?"

"What?"

He was busy dialing. "I'm running a fever, and you're Lori Martin."

"I don—" But he had shoved the phone to me.

"Brevard High School, main office," a crisp, business voice said in my ear, "How may I direct your call?"

"Um, attendance office please."

"One moment."

I put my hand over the mouthpiece. "Dominic, I w—oh, hi...lo, um," I removed my hand and cleared my throat, "Hello. This is Lori Martin. Dominic is sick."

"Dominic is sick?"

"Yes, he's, um, running a fever."

"Another fever?"

"Yes," I said, "Another one." I bit my lip.

"Remind him to bring a note and check in at the office when he returns to school."

"I will," I said. "Good-bye." I snapped the phone shut and glared at him. "Don't ever do that again!"

"What, you expect me to call for you, but you won't call for me?"

"Yes, no, I mean—" I took a breath. "Yes, I'll call for you, but you have to give me a minute, not just shove the phone in my ear!"

"Clearly," he said. "You sucked."

"I know," I said miserably. "Think they know?"

Dominic was picking up the kitchen phone. "What's your dad's name?"

"Heinrich."

"Heinrich? Wow."

"What?"

He was dialing. "Just one happy German family, aren't you?"

"Actually, my mom is Canadian."

"Attendance office, please." He looked at me and then rolled his eyes. "Whatever," he mouthed at me. "Hi, this is Heinrich Reichard, and I'm calling to let you know that my daughter

Silke won't be in class today. She woke up with a sore throat…. Yeah, something's going around already…. Great….And can we get her assignments sent to the office?…. Thank you."

He hung up.

"You're pretty good at that."

"Experience pays, baby. It's better than books."

"You are so corny."

"Are we going or what?"

"Yeah," I said with a smile. "Let's go."

* * *

Dominic steered me into the coffee shop. "I need caffeine," he said. "I don't function well without it."

"Okay." I wasn't in a hurry. We had hours to get the groceries and take them back to the house. It was a beautiful fall morning, and I felt new and free. I was smiling as Dominic opened the door for me and waited for me to enter first.

People stared at us while we walked up to the coffee bar, and I felt familiar panic grab my stomach with both fists. We were supposed to be in school. Would people call the cops? Did people report truants? My mother would.

But at the register, as Dominic placed the order, I realized that the old lady putting sugar in her coffee was staring at his head. I had gotten so comfortable around him that I had forgotten how freaky he looked.

We took our drinks to a small table by the window. Dominic dropped his wallet and I scooped it up.

"Give it back," he said.

"I will. I just wanna see—" I flipped it open and gasped. "No way!" I looked up at him and then back at the wallet and shrieked.

"Shhhshhhshh!" He hissed. "Give it back!" He was turning red. I pulled his student ID out of the main plastic sleeve and tossed his wallet to him.

"Oh my God!"

"Silke—"

"Oh. My. God." I yanked the card away as he lunged across the table, trying to snatch it back. "McNair Academy?"

"I told you that."

"No," I said, shaking my head, "You said *a* private school."

"Exactly. McNair is—"

"McNair is *the* private school!" A private boarding school, one that president's kids went to, one that sent all of their graduates to Ivy League schools, one that had polo and fencing teams, one that was completely unlike Brevard High School.

"I can't believe you went there!" was what I said. *I can't believe how hot you are*, was what I was thinking. In the ID, he was wearing a dark grey jacket that stretched across his shoulders; the McNair crest was embroidered in gold on his light grey tie. His gorgeous green eyes that hypnotized me now, were mesmerizing when framed with his naturally dark, short cropped hair, and—"You used mousse!"

"Give it back!" He growled.

I couldn't stop looking back and forth between the ID card hunk in my hand and the rainbowed friend on the other side of the table. The high cheekbones and straight nose were the same, and the eyes were same color...but they were different too. In the picture, Dominic looked like he was excited to take on the world, like he knew a secret no one else did. Now— ever since I had known him, I realized—he looked haunted, mistrustful, like he was waiting for the next kick to come.

"What happened?"

He set his jaw and held out his hand. Reluctantly, I returned the ID card. I wanted to keep it and sleep with it under my pillow.

"What happened?" I asked again when it became apparent he was ignoring me.

He lifted one shoulder and then dropped it. "Money got tight. Even with the scholarship, and living at home, we couldn't afford the textbooks and activity fees."

There was something he wasn't telling me. "But—"

His phone began playing 'You Are My Sunshine.' He started cursing like a criminal, and snatched it up from the table. People were staring again, he was so loud and obscene.

"Let's go," he muttered, shoving the phone in his pocket where it continued to sing. Dominic pushed back from the table, letting his chair fall over with a crash.

I stood up and hurriedly gathered our half empty cups and napkins, putting them in the trash before I trotted after him.

I caught up to him on the sidewalk.

"Busted! God! I'm busted! I *knew* I should have gone to school today!"

My heart sank. We had been caught, and it was my fault. His phone gave a series of tones, and he grimaced, closed his eyes and shook his head, bouncing on his toes.

"Dominic—"

He took a few steps, spun on his heel, took a couple more, and then stopped when his phone beeped incessantly at him. He flipped the top open and sighed. "I've got to go."

"I'm sorry," I said miserably.

"It's not your fault," he said.

"Yes it is. I'll come with you."

"No, go to the grocery store, get the stuff you need."

"Maybe it won't be so bad if we go in now."

He frowned at me. "What do you mean?"

"Maybe they'll only give us one or two days of detention."

Dominic stared at me blankly for a few seconds, then he burst out laughing. "It wasn't the attendance police, Silke."

"Oh," I said, feeling stupid and relieved at the same time.

"You're priceless, you know that?"

The off-handed compliment made me feel warm, even though it shouldn't have. "Then what's going on?"

"I've got to go," he said again.

"Can I come with you?"

I could tell by the way he started to take a breath that he was going to say no. But then he stopped and said, "Sure. Why not?"

His phone beeped again. "Arrgh. We've got to go now, though. No time for grocery shopping."

I shrugged. "Okay."

"Ready to run?"

"What?"

"We've got four minutes to get to Broadway and Central."

My eyebrows went up. "Not gonna happen."

He grinned. "Better make it happen."

We stared at each other for another three seconds, then both turned and bolted as if we had been counting out loud.

Four minutes later, we ran up to the bus stop on Broadway and Central. "Crap," Dominic gasped, bending over and grabbing his knees to hold himself up. "We missed it."

"No—" I took a breath and it burned. "We didn't!"

He saw the bus rumbling down the street towards us and a smile lit up his face. "We made it."

"I'm not sure—" I was still struggling for air. "—I think...I may have dropped a few internal organs back there."

"We'll check for them on the way home," he said as we climbed on the bus. "Man, I don't think I've run that far in a year!"

"I've never run that far," I retorted, dropping in the seat.

"Really? Then you should go out for track. You're good."

"I'm not going to be able to walk tomorrow."

"That's okay, I'm not going to be able to walk tonight. You'll have to carry me home."

"Where are we going, anyway? Who busted you?"

"My mom," Dominic said, looking down at his phone. He still hadn't opened it to check any of the messages. "She knows I'm not in school."

"How do you know that she knows that? Maybe she was just calling to tell you to pick up some milk on the way home."

A strange look crossed his face. "Not a chance. So who are we going to get notes from?"

"What?"

"Well, we're both missing Norton's class. How are we going to get the notes?"

I didn't know why he wanted to change the subject, but I figured that I had caused enough trouble for one day, so I went along with it. "We'll have to ask someone."

"Think Bridget will bail us out a second time?"

"No," I said, loving the way he said us. "But we can probably get the notes from Daisy."

"How about you get the notes from her, and then I get them from you?"

"You don't trust her notes?"

He shrugged. "I like the way you put curls on your g's."

It was a longer bus ride than I had expected. We went all the way to the heart of the city and then kept going. Finally, on the far side, we got off the bus.

And transferred to another one.

That broke my resolve. "Where, exactly, are we going?"

"Just a bit further. Why are you in Spanish, anyway? Shouldn't you be taking German?"

I accepted the topic change again. We'd get where we were going eventually.

We got off the bus on the south side, in front of the hospital. As the bus pulled away, Dominic sat down on the bench.

I sighed and sat down next to him. Another bus ride.

He bent over his knees for a moment, and when he sat up straight again, he had cuffed his pants up, hiding the frayed ends that usually dragged under his heels. Then he started buttoning his flannel shirt, covering the stained t-shirt he wore under it.

"What are you doing?" I asked.

He didn't answer as he unrolled his sleeves, and buttoned them neatly at his wrists. Then he began undoing his ponytails, one at a time.

"Dominic?"

But he kept working his hair, until finally all six of the rubber bands were in a pile on his lap. He ran his fingers through the multi-colored locks, and smoothed them into one low ponytail, in the traditional spot at the nape of his neck.

And the only color that showed now was dark brown with white ends. I knew it was his natural color because I had just seen it in the ID card.

He stood up in front of me, tucking his shirt in. Just like that, he utterly transformed from a freak to a handsome, preppy lumberjack.

"Ready?" he rumbled.

"For what?" I asked. Something serious was coming, that was clear. But I had no idea what.

"To meet my mom," he said, and he walked to the hospital door.

CHAPTER FOURTEEN

"Dominic!" I wanted to yell at him, but the quiet hush in the hospital sucked the air out of my lungs. I was almost afraid to run after him, but I was more afraid of losing him and not knowing where he was going.

He stopped in front of the elevator and jabbed the up button. I gritted my teeth and decided to wait until we were in the elevator to let him have it. But by the time the bell rang and the doors slid open, there were four other people behind us, and one of them was a doctor. Two more people hurried in just before the doors closed.

The elevator stopped at the second, third, and fourth floors, but by the time we got out on the fifth floor, we had more people in it than we started with I followed him down the white hall. The walls were white and shiny, and the floor tiles were white and shiny, and the ceiling was white. If it had been shiny too, it would have been like being inside an egg.

Dominic slouched with the same confident purpose he always had, and we passed door after door and even another hallway. But then he slowed down a little, and I caught up to him. He took a deep breath and put his shoulders back, then took my hand and smiled. His eyes were overly bright. He gave my hand a tug, and we went into the last room on the left.

The room was white, of course, but the olive green curtain that divided the room in two was almost cheery. Two small, framed prints, the kind that Wal-Mart sells by the millions, were on the wall opposite the beds. I was pretty sure staring at them all day would only increase patient depression.

There was an old man in the bed closest the door. He was reading a book and looked up with a hopeful expression on his face, but when he saw us, he scowled and looked back at his book without saying anything.

Dominic smiled brightly and said, "Morning, Mr. Conrad, how's things?" Mr. Conrad only pursed his lips and turned a page.

"Dominic, my sunshine, you're here!"

We rounded the flimsy curtain. Dominic's mother lay on her bed, a non-hospital yellow and red checked blanket tucked around her shoulders. On the wall next to her were four drawings, three on white paper and one on lined paper that had been pulled from a spiral notebook, and a framed picture sat on top of the beeping machine next to her. If I hadn't seen Dominic's old ID card, I would have wondered who it was.

Dominic gave my hand a brief squeeze and then dropped it. "Of course I'm here, Mom. You called."

"And you didn't answer," she said. I could tell she was trying to look severe, but even with dark shadows under her eyes and pale cheeks, her eyes sparkled.

Dominic leaned over and kissed her cheek. "Figured you'd rather yell at me in person instead."

"Hmmm," she said in the way that mothers do to let you know they're not happy with you, but they're not really mad, either. "And who is this? Who have you found that's smart enough to see through the hairy disguise you've been wearing lately?"

"I'm Silke Reichard," I said, stepping forward to the foot of her bed. "Dominic and I have Western Civ together."

"It's nice to meet you, Silke. I'm Lori. I'm glad Dominic's got someone smart to help him with social studies. Maybe you can help him stop being so difficult."

"I think that would take psychology. Years of it."

"Hey!" Dominic said indignantly.

Lori leaned her head back and laughed. "I like you!"

"Then maybe you can keep her," Dominic muttered.

Lori reached out and grabbed Dominic's hand. "Oh, no. You're the one I'm keeping! My darling Dominic!"

Dominic grimaced. "So you called?"

"Yes," she said, pressing a button so the bed hummed as it raised her to a more upright position. Dominic helped her shift her pillows around and then tucked her blanket around her. When she was settled, I could tell her breathing took effort, and a sheen had broken out on her forehead. "Sit down. Both of you," she added as I took a small step back.

I really felt like I should leave and let the two of them talk. "I could go—"

"Sit!" Lori said sharply.

I got the chair from the corner of the room, and pulled it over to the side of her bed. Dominic pulled the chair next to her bed even closer, next to her shoulder.

"You're supposed to be in school."

Dominic looked down at his feet.

"Dom? Where were you?"

"Helping me," I said quickly. "I had to, uh—" I cast around, trying to think of something that would have pulled me out of school and required help. "To, uh, help—"

"She's a good listener, Mom. I needed to talk."

Lori lifted her hand and traced Dominic's cheek. "I'm sorry," she said softly.

Dominic swallowed and shook his head.

"But," she continued with a stronger voice, "That's not a reason to skip school. The attendance clerk told me that you've already missed five days of school! It hasn't even been two weeks yet!"

"I nee—"

Lori raised her hand abruptly, cutting him off. "You've missed five days of school *and* you've helped yourself to store supplies *and* you've been out past curfew."

"You've been talking to Ivy," Dominic grumbled.

"Of course I have! You can't really expect me to leave you alone just because I'm in the hospital!"

"You shouldn't be worrying. You need to rest."

"I'm your mother. It's my job to worry. And you're abusing Ivy," she said.

Dominic looked up. "I am not!"

"You're abusing her kind nature," his mother said quietly. "She knows how upset and hurt you are, so she's bending over backwards to be nice to you. I told her to quit babying you. From now on, you're to be home on time and in school every day."

Instead of arguing, Dominic said, "I'm sorry."

"Otherwise," Lori continued as if he hadn't said anything. "You will get a hair cut and move to Oregon."

"Ha!"

"Even if I have to shave your head myself," she said.

"You couldn't—"

"Don't test me, Dom. I'll sit on you if I have to. And you'll go live with your father. He's worried about you, too."

Dominic snorted.

"He knows as well as I do what you're doing, you know."

"Whatever."

Lori simply stared at him. It wasn't a glare like my mom would have given me; it was more of an expression that said 'I know you can figure this out.'

"I'll be good," Dominic muttered.

"Oh, you've always been good," his mom said. "The question is, will you behave?"

"I'll behave."

"Thank you. Now. Let's see the hair. Come on," she said when he hesitated, "Ivy said you'd done something new."

Slowly Dominic reached back and pulled out the rubber band, shaking his hair out.

"Come on, come on," she said, "Let me see."

Dominic leaned forward over her bed. Lori's slender fingers parted and pulled his hair.

"Hmmm," she said, inspecting the silver tips, "You did a good job with the highlights. Much better than the blue when you first added it."

"Silke helped me."

"Really?" Lori looked over Dominic's tangled rainbow and

smiled at me. "Are you interested in cosmetology?"

"I don't know what I'm interested in."

"You're a ninth grader too?"

I nodded.

"Then it's probably better to keep your options open anyway. That's what I keep telling this one." She pushed Dominic's head away.

He reached up and began finger combing his hair back into the tidy ponytail.

"Would you like anything from the cafeteria?" I asked quickly. "I could go—"

"You both need to go," she interrupted. "I'm getting tired and I have a treatment later today."

I stood up quickly.

"I'll come back this afternoon," Dominic said.

"No, don't do that. Stay home and do your schoolwork. Come back tomorrow night with Ivy."

"But—"

"It's going to be rough today," she said quietly. "I can feel it. Please stay home."

Dominic sighed. "Okay." He lifted her hand and kissed it. "If that's—"

"What I really want," she finished with him. "It is. Stay home tonight. Call if you'd like."

He nodded and stood up. "I will, Mom. I love you."

"Love you too," she said.

Dominic leaned over and kissed her cheek. "You sure?"

"Positive."

He walked slowly toward the green curtain where I was standing.

"Oh, wait," she said suddenly.

Dominic spun on his heel and was back to her side in less than three steps. "Yes?"

"I almost forgot," she said, trying to push herself up even more. "It's over there," she pointed to the nightstand behind her machine. "In the top drawer."

Dominic opened the drawer. "Mom—"

"Now, now," she said, "Put it on."

Dominic pulled out a baseball hat. He put it on his head and grinned. "Thanks."

"They're still your favorite team, right?" she asked anxiously. "You haven't changed sides, have you?"

"Once a Redwing, always a Redwing, you know that, Mom."

He kissed her cheek again, knocking the hat sideways in the process, and then we left.

"It was nice to meet you, Silke!" she called weakly as I walked out the door.

"You, too," I called back.

As soon as we were in the hallway, Dominic said, "Hold this," and he handed me his new hat.

"Redwings?"

"Hockey team."

"Oh yeah."

Dominic untucked his shirt and then began working on the buttons. By the time we reached the elevator, the flannel shirt was unbuttoned and the sleeves were rolled up. In the elevator, he pulled the rubber band out of his hair again, and then took the hat from me. He settled it firmly on his head—backward—and proceeded to pull a thick lock out through the loop, so a shank of brown, green, and red hair dangled over his eyes.

From hunk to freak, just like that.

"Who are you hiding?" I asked as the elevator doors slid open. "Who is the persona? Who is the real you?"

As the hospital doors whooshed open, he said, "All of 'em."

*   *   *

It was sunny, but there was a breeze blowing and when we were in the shadows, I tried not to shiver. We were quiet while we waited for the bus, and quiet on the ride back. I was waiting for him to talk. After all, he had told Lori I was a good listener. Plus I was afraid to say anything; I didn't want to say the wrong thing.

It seemed like it was a shorter bus ride back than it had been to get there. At the bus stop, Dominic said, "Grocery store?"

I shook my head. "It's too late." I wasn't positive what time Mom and Dad would get home, and there was absolutely no way I was going anywhere near my street, let alone into my house, now.

"Aw, Silke, I'm sorry. We should have done that first."

"No," I said firmly, "It was much more important to go see your mom." Since he looked like he was going to argue, I added, "Dad'll go shopping tomorrow anyway—and maybe the excitement of Vegas will leave confusion about what was in the fridge."

"Um. Now what?"

"Milkshakes?"

His face lit up. "Yeah. That's perfect."

As we walked to the diner, I said, "So what's wrong?"

"Kidney failure."

"Oh."

"Not her fault, though. She was in a car accident a couple years ago, really bad. She lost one kidney outright, and then this one's become the victim of Rhabdomyolysis," he pronounced the word very carefully. I figured he knew what it meant, but I didn't ask; I was sure it was a technical explanation for why she was sick. And really, when your mom was suffering in the hospital, did it matter what kept her there?

"Is she going to have surgery?"

"She's not on the donor list yet."

"Why not?" I demanded. It was clear to me she was really sick. In fact, I thought she looked like she was dying.

"The insurance company is refusing to pay. It's ironic, in a sad sort of way. She was hit by a drunk driver, and now she's the one dying of kidney failure even though she's never been much of a drinker."

"That's awful."

He snorted.

We ordered French fries and milkshakes—strawberry for him and caramel for me—and sat in a corner booth.

"So what did your mom mean about your dad?"

"He wants me to come live with him, so I won't be a 'burden' on Mom while she's 'coping with this thing.' He doesn't understand why I think being a thousand miles away from her would be bad. He thinks talking on the phone is just as good as seeing someone in person. After all, it's worked for him for the last nine years." Dominic scowled at a French fry and ripped it in half.

"His wife isn't crazy about having me come live with them," he continued, "But she can handle it as long as I'm a well-behaved, well-groomed young man."

"As long as you're a McNair honor student," I said.

"Exactly. I highlighted my hair, last Thanksgiving I think it was, and she completely freaked. So when Dad started leaning on me to move out there—"

"You dyed your hair green."

"Actually, blue was first," he said with a grin, "Just the bangs. But it was enough to make her refuse to let me move in. 'Not until he gets his act together,'" he said in a sing-song voice. "'Not until he stops looking like a Martian.'"

"Obviously she doesn't think Martin Martian's are cute."

"Do you?"

I choked on my milkshake.

"Anyway," Dominic calmly went on while I was gasping for air, "I thought Ivy and I had a sweet deal going. She's working a lot of hours and she's really never been much of a maternal type. We agreed that I'd stay out of trouble and she'd stay out of my way. She's gonna get the store when Mom goes, and I didn't think she'd be willing to add to Mom's stress. Guess I underestimated her."

"Maybe she just realized that if something happened to you, it would add to everyone's stress."

Dominic shrugged.

"You're amazing."

His eyes widened. "What? Why?"

I felt myself blush, but I pushed on anyway. "Your mom is in the hospital. Your dad lives in another state. You're practically living on your own. You don't care what anyone else thinks. And you're brilliant."

He tilted his head and a smile spread slowly across his face. "You got one of them wrong."

I put my chin on my hand and said, "Oh really?"

"I'm super brilliant." I rolled my eyes. He stood up and asked, "Ready to go?"

I checked my watch. "Yeah. I gotta go get Grete."

"Nice alliteration."

"Thanks," I said as I got to my feet.

"Next time add some onomatopoeia."

"Sure."

"See? Super brilliant."

"I know what onomatopoeia is. So I guess I'm super brilliant too."

"If you're only guessing, then you're not super brilliant. If you're super brilliant, you *know* you're super brilliant."

I tried to elbow him but he sidled out of my way.

We walked to my neighborhood together, just chatting. I thought about reaching out to take his hand, the way he had so casually taken mine before, but I just couldn't find the nerve.

"Think you know your way from here?"

"Um, unless I've just become super stupid instead of super brilliant, then yeah, I know my way."

"Good."

"Tell her I said hi."

"Tell who?"

"You're going back to the hospital, aren't you?"

"Of course."

"So tell her I said hi."

He smiled. "I will. And I'll see you at school tomorrow. No more cutting class for you!"

"And no more getting suspended for you!"

"I told you, I wasn't suspended. I was—"

"I know," I said, shoving him on his shoulder. "I know." I started walking to Pioneer.

"Hey Silke," Dominic called.

I turned back around.

"You're not super brilliant!"

"Thanks."

"You got something else wrong, too."

"Oh yeah? What's that?"

"I do care what people think. If that people is you."

We were standing nearly twenty feet apart, but it was like I could feel his breath against my skin.

He turned to walk away, and so did I.

CHAPTER FIFTEEN

"How are my girls?" Dad called from the kitchen as we walked in the front door.

"Daddy!" Grete squealed, running full speed.

I practically ran down the hall to Grete's room to drop off her bag. She had been super happy when I picked her up at school, and when I offered to carry her over-night bag home, she didn't even ask why I didn't have my school pack.

I took a deep breath before I hurried back to the kitchen.

"What, didn't you miss us, too?" Dad asked, swinging me into a hug. "Had to go to your room first?"

"Just taking all our stuff to our rooms," I said. I was trying to look normal and not glare at him and accuse him of hat rigging. "How was your trip?"

"Fantastic," he said. "Just the way it was supposed to be. There's so much stuff there now for kids, like roller coasters and arcades, that we should probably take you two next time."

"Hooray!" Grete clapped her hands and jumped up and down.

"Great," I said, thinking that maybe it would have been okay if one of the 'Go to Vegas' slips had accidentally fallen into my hat after all.

"Grete, what did you get on the back of your pants?"

"Someone painted the merry-go-round, and we didn't know the paint was still wet."

Mom grumbled something as she turned to the fridge and Dad was inspecting Grete's pants, so neither of them saw me choke back a laugh.

"What happened to all the milk?" Mom asked, closing the refrigerator door.

"Oh, I threw it out Friday morning," I said, trying to sound careless. "It tasted funny."

She shook her head. "Dad just bought it last week. I'm sure it was fine."

"It smelled."

"I'll go grocery shopping tomorrow," Dad said easily. "Start a list."

Mom sighed but came around the island and stopped short. "What did you do to your hair?"

"I got a new look," I grinned, but she didn't.

"How could I have missed that?" Dad said. "Turn around, let me get a good look."

Obediently I spun slowly.

"Nice," he said, nodding.

Mom reached out and ran her fingers through my bangs, then she shook her head. "It's not going to be fun growing those out. They're going to be in your eyes."

"Who says I want to grow them out?"

"It's really not a good look for your face, Silke. You're much better off with the same length you've always had."

"I like it," I said stubbornly. "I'm going to keep it, for a while, at least."

"Well you're going to have to," Mom said irritably. "It's going to take a while for them to grow out. I can't believe Janet would let you cut your hair like that."

Dad intervened, "Speaking of, did you have a good weekend at Alexi's?"

"No."

"No?" Dad's eyebrows went up in surprise. "How could you and Alexi *not* have a good time together?"

"She had surgery on Friday."

Mom and Dad both exploded with shocked and concerned questions.

I held up my hand. "She's fine now. She had to have her appendix removed."

"Oh, good, at least it was something simple," Dad said.

"Poor Janet," Mom said. "Having a daughter in the hospital

and watching a friend at the same time! She must have been going crazy!"

"Well, actually, I didn't stay with them."

Mom froze. "What?"

"I didn't want to cause anymore stress for Mrs. Amerman, so I stayed with Bridget instead."

Mom cocked her head. "You didn't call me? Janet didn't call me?"

"Teresa, you lost your phone—" Dad began while I said, "Everything was fine. We didn't want to wreck your weekend."

"But I don't know Bridget. Or her parents."

"I know," I said, "But it was last minute, and you left your cell phones. It all worked out. Everything is fine. No big deal."

"No big deal?" Mom practically shrieked. "You spent the weekend with strangers and it's no big deal?"

"Mom—" I tried while Dad said, "Teresa—"

"How could you do that? What were you thinking? What was Janet thinking? Strangers! I might as well have just left you home alone for the weekend!"

My stomach convulsed like I'd been hit.

"Teresa," Dad said again, firmly. "Calm down. Silke made a reasonable decision—"

"Ha! Reasonable?"

"—dealing with an emergency situation. She's fine."

"But—" Mom snapped her mouth shut so fast I actually heard her teeth click. "They let her cut her hair! What else did they let her do? We've never even met them!"

"She's fine," Dad repeated. Mom turned her back to us, staring out the window.

"Do you want to talk to Mr. or Mrs. Ulbricht?" I asked, trying to ignore the pounding in my ears. "I could call and—" I had my cell phone open, knowing that Dominic would understand what was going on as soon as I called him Mr. Ulbricht.

"That's okay," Dad said, but he never took his eyes off

Mom. "Do you have any homework?"

"Yeah," I said, though I had no idea if I did or not.

"Grete?"

"Yes," she said, looking at Mom with big eyes. She hadn't said a word the whole time and I had almost forgotten she was in the room.

"Why don't you both go get to work? We'll call you when dinner's ready."

Grete didn't need to be told twice. She slid off the chair and left the kitchen, and I was right behind her.

She hesitated outside her bedroom door. "Why is Mommy so upset?"

I have no idea, I thought. "She just wants to make sure we're safe," I said, trying to sound reassuring. I tugged on one of her curls, getting her to grin at me before she slipped into her room.

I turned my phone off with a pang. I wanted Dominic to call, but I didn't want all my friends calling, asking why I hadn't been at school.

The rest of the evening passed quickly. I finished my math and science from Friday, and did the next two pages of math exercises, hoping that they had been assigned today. Then I spent nearly a half hour trying to forge Dad's signature for the attendance office. I wasn't happy with any of them, so I shredded all of them.

Dinner was a little awkward. Mom barely talked and she hardly looked directly at me. Dad explained that she had lost her phone at the airport, and was a little stressed about it because it had all of her contacts in it. I tried to seem relaxed and normal, and since no one said anything, I guess I did.

Before I went to bed, I checked my messages. I had one from Bridget, Daisy, and Emma, and three from Alexi. But none from Dominic.

*　　　　　*　　　　　*

"Oh my God!" Alexi squealed when she saw me at our corner the next morning. "You look so cute!"

"Thanks," I said with a grin, running my fingers through my bangs and fluffing them a little more.

"What did everyone else say about it?"

"Um—"

"I bet Jason thought it was really cute!"

"Um—"

"Sorry I didn't call to tell you yesterday," she went on, "I just really wasn't ready to walk around all day, you know? So I asked Mom if I could stay home one more day and she said okay, just like that! She had to go to work, of course, so I got to spend the whole day on the couch watching movies. It was great! So what'd I miss?"

I was still trying to catch up with her rambling. "Wait. You didn't go to school yesterday?"

"Well, duh! Didn't you notice?"

"I didn't go either," I said.

"Why? Were you sick?"

"No," I said slowly, "I just didn't feel like going."

"Wow. And your mom let you stay?"

I didn't say anything right away.

"Wait a minute," Alexi said, "Your mom wasn't home yesterday."

"Nope."

Alexi stopped and grabbed my arm, making me stop too. "What's going on, Silke?"

"I don't—"

"Exactly, you don't. You don't call me, you don't come see me, you don't answer my email, and now you're saying you don't go to school?"

"I missed a day, Alexi. It's no big deal."

Alexi was shaking her head. "There's something you're not telling me. You're hiding something."

"Come on," I said, shaking off her hand, "We're going to be late."

We didn't talk any more while we walked to school, and I could tell she was upset with me.

Inside, I turned to head to our lockers, but she grabbed my arm again. Before I could say anything, though, she said, "Admit slip?"

"Oh, yeah, thanks," I said.

With each step closer to the attendance office, my throat seemed to tighten a little bit more. I felt like I could hardly breathe by the time we got there. There was a line of five students in front of us. When we got to the front, Alexi stepped aside, making me go first, which was probably good, because if I had to wait much longer, I'd probably vomit and then choke on it since my throat was so tight.

"Silke Reichard," I said.

"Do you have a note?" Mrs. Shive barked as she scanned a computer printout in front of her.

"My dad called yesterday but forgot to write a note this mo—"

"Ah, that's right, he wanted your assignments sent down here. We don't do that unless a student is absent for more than two days." She was scribbling on a piece of paper. "Get it signed by all your teachers and bring it back before you leave school. Next!"

I was afraid I'd cry with relief if I said anything, so I merely bobbed my head as I took the paper and moved to let Alexi step up to the desk.

"Alexi Amerman," she said quietly.

"Oh, yes," Mrs. Shive actually stopped writing and looked up. "It was your appendix, right? How are you feeling, dear?"

"Fine, thanks," Alexi mumbled.

When we walked out of the office together, Alexi glared at me. "I can't believe you got away with that!"

"Shh!" I hissed, looking over my shoulder in terror, but Mrs. Shive was focused on the next student.

"Unbelievable."

"Are you mad because I cut yesterday or because I didn't get caught?" I asked as we climbed the stairs.

"I'm mad because you're not acting like my best friend."

"It's one day, Alexi. Let it go."

She looked at me out of the corner of her eye, but didn't say anything else as we got our books from our lockers and split up for class.

*   *   *

"What's the word of the week?" Alexi asked as we sat down for lunch.

"Unperturbed," I said, scanning the cafeteria. I hadn't seen Dominic all day. I wanted to warn him that he might have to play Mr. Ulbricht for me one more time.

"Unperturbed?" Emma repeated.

"Yeah, as in he was unperturbed all weekend."

"I liked amok better."

"No!" I said, a little too sharply based on Alexi's expression. "We can't repeat. If you don't like unperturbed, how about stoic?"

"I sense a theme," Danny said, smiling.

Just a few days ago, having Danny smile at me specifically would have reduced me to a puddle on the floor. Today, I hardly noticed. "I wasn't trying to be sly," I said.

"Something on your mind, Silke?" Bridget asked.

"Yeah, Silke, tell us what's going on. What's *really* going on," Alexi said.

"Just the same old-same old. You know, getting crap from my friends," I replied, trying to keep my tone light.

"Maybe you wouldn't get crap if you quit hiding things from them." The tension between Alexi and me must have been apparent to the rest of the table. "We know that unperturbed and stoic don't refer to you, so who are you thinking about?"

"Did you meet someone special at the mall this weekend?" Bridget teased.

"Nice earrings," I said.

"Thanks," she replied, tilting her head to show the daisies on her earlobes. "Got them shopping this weekend."

"You went to the mall this weekend?" Alexi asked.

"Yeah," Bridget and I said together. Bridget launched into a re-telling of our shopping, something that I usually would join in, but today completely bored me. Abruptly I pushed back from the table and left. I didn't pick up my tray or turn around when Daisy and Alexi called after me.

We weren't supposed to wander the halls during lunch, which I had never thought about before. Today it seemed like one more pointless rule. When the security guard asked where I was going, I told her I had to talk to a teacher and then just kept wandering.

I was much more anxious going to Western Civ that day than I had been on the first day of school. I sat in my regular chair, the only person in my row now.

"Mr. Martin is gone again, I see. Perhaps the office forgot to send me his withdrawal notice," Mr. Norton said as he entered attendance in the computer.

"He's planning on coming back," I said clearly. "There's just a lot of serious stuff he has to deal with right now."

Mr. Norton looked at me with almost sympathetic eyes. "I'm afraid that Mr. Martin's stuff is only going to get more serious."

I dutifully took notes all hour, making sure to curl my g's neatly for Dominic.

After school, I waited for Alexi, but she never came to her locker. I walked home alone for the first time since second grade.

*   *   *

While I was waiting for Grete, I called Alexi. It went straight to voice mail. "Hey, Alexi," I said, stopping to clear my throat. "I'm sorry about today. I really need to talk to you. A lot of things happened this weekend, and I need someone to talk to.

I know I can trust you to listen and help me out. Please give me a call when you get this."

I hung up and then called Dominic. It just wasn't my day. His phone went to voice mail too. "Hey, Dominic, give me a call and I'll go over our social studies assignment with you," I said. I hesitated and then just hung up. I didn't know what else to say.

Everything else was normal. Grete and I walked home and had a snack. She started her homework right away, just like we were supposed to. Just like I used to do. Today, I turned on the radio and flopped on the bed. Things felt unhinged. I searched my thoughts, but they were murky and I couldn't find a focus.

Dad came home. Grete joined him in the kitchen. I grabbed a book and pretended to read. I could hear the muffled sounds of them talking, and of cabinets being opened and closed.

I couldn't believe how easy it had been. I hadn't ever skipped a class before, let alone a whole day. I had never spent a night by myself, let alone a whole weekend. I had never lied to my parents or teachers or friends.

And I had gotten away with it all.

I should have been celebrating; I should have been smiling and having fun and joking around. But I was miserable.

Everything felt false. I had done so much this weekend—done things I never would have dreamed of before—and I felt the changes it was working on me. But I was stuffing everything away, trying to go back to who I was just three days ago, and it was uncomfortable.

It was suffocating.

In a very strange sort of way, I wanted to be caught. I wanted someone else to know that I was different, so I could continue to be different.

"Silke?"

I jumped. Dad was standing in my bedroom doorway, watching me. "What are you doing?"

I glanced at the book lying next to me. When had I put it down? "Just thinking."

"Anything in particular?"

"No. Not really."

"Why don't you join us? We put the casserole in and we're going to make some cookie dough to bake after dinner."

The last thing I wanted to do today was bake cookies. "I think I'll just read."

"You sure?"

"Yeah," I said.

He looked like he was going to say something else, but then he kind of nodded and left.

I closed my eyes. I wanted to be different, but I hated the fact that I saw my father differently now.

How could he have cheated on the hat? How long had he been cheating? Had he cheated on other things too?

He had been the one I trusted most, the one I always felt I could talk to. And now I was afraid to talk to him, because I knew that sooner or later, I'd have to ask. I'd have to know. Why? Why had he rigged the hat?

I looked at the book again and then shook my head. No way was I going to be able to focus enough to read. I walked down the hall to the office and turned on the computer.

I skimmed all the chatter. This was stuff that mattered to my friends, and even yesterday it mattered to me, but today I just couldn't care. Alexi was already off-line, so I couldn't try to have a private chat with her. It was too close to dinner to try to call her; I needed more time to talk to her than just few minutes. I went to search for friends, and entered Dominic Martin. Again I narrowed the search to our city, and then I skimmed through the photos.

This time I found him, because his profile pic was the same as his McNair ID card. I clicked on him, but of course he restricted his access. So I sent him a friend request. I went to my profile and updated my status: No longer color blinded.

I smiled as I signed off. That kind of cryptic status would drive Alexi and Emma nuts.

"SILKE!"

I jumped up and hurried to the kitchen. I must have really been into what I was doing, because I hadn't heard anyone call before, but from the tone of Mom's shout, she had probably yelled my name at least twice already.

"Sorry, sorry," I said, skidding around the corner into the kitchen. "I didn't hear you. I'll get the table set and—" I broke off. Mom and Dad were standing by the island, and Mom looked furious. Dad looked confused and concerned.

"Explain yourself!" Mom snapped.

Bewildered, I looked from Mom to Dad and back to Mom. "What?"

"Oh, you know what!"

The problem was, I had too many things that she may have found out about. I wasn't about to incriminate myself. "Really, Mom," I said, eyes wide, "I don't know what you're talking about."

"I just took the garbage out." She paused significantly, but it meant nothing to me. I glanced at Dad and he looked baffled too. "There was already a fair amount of garbage in there." She paused again, and when I shook my head, she slammed her fist on the counter. "Including empty Chinese boxes and a pizza box."

"Was it supposed to go in the recycling bin?" I asked.

"It was delivered here on Friday night."

I stared at her. My mind was blank. I wasn't even trying and rejecting excuses or reasons; I couldn't seem to think at all.

"Are you sure?" Dad asked.

Mom made a strange strangling sound and ground out, "The delivery sticker on the pizza box says Friday, August 26."

Dad looked at me. "Did you and Alexi have dinner here Friday night?"

"Alexi had surgery Friday afternoon!" Mom exploded. "*Alexi* wasn't here! But *Silke* was here. She wasn't supposed to be here, but she was." Mom drew a jagged breath. "And she *lied* to us about it."

"Silke?" Dad looked at me. "Do you have anything to say?"

"No," I said, "Not really." And it was weird. I had been so stressed about getting caught last night that I felt ill. But now that I had been caught, I felt almost serene. The blood wasn't pounding in my ears, my chest didn't feel tight, my stomach wasn't threatening to empty itself; I just was.

"No?" Mom demanded. "You have nothing to say?"

"I had pizza here Friday night," I said calmly. "I had to wait until Mr. Ulbricht could get off work and then come pick me up."

"How long were you here by yourself?" Dad asked.

I shrugged. "I don't know," I said. "It really wasn't any big deal."

"Okay," Dad said. "You should have told us about it, but—"

"She lied! Nothing is okay, nothing at all!"

"Teresa," Dad began in his soothing tone.

Mom moved around the island, coming toward me. "You lied!" she shouted, pointing her finger practically in my face. "After all we've taught you—"

"After all I've done!" I yelled back. I mean really yelled. It actually shut her up. "Straight A's all my life, never had detention, never talked back, never did anything wrong, and after all that, you *still* won't let me do anything! I got a cute conservative haircut, and all you can talk about is how fast it'll grow back to the way I've lived my whole life! You act like I'm some sort of delinquent who can't be trusted!"

"You lied! Why should we trust you?" Mom yelled back.

"Maybe because I've never lied before? I've *always* been responsible! I take care of Grete for you, and you won't even give me an allowance! I get all my homework done every night, and you still won't let me watch more than an hour of TV!"

"And as soon as we give you an inch—"

"Yeah, I took a mile! I stayed home by myself and *ordered a pizza*! I didn't have a wild party! I didn't even open a beer! I stayed home, I ate pizza, and I cleaned up after myself! Damn, why haven't you thrown me in jail yet?"

"Don't you talk to me that way!" Mom practically screamed.

"Great idea!" I screamed back. "I won't talk to you at all!" I whirled around and headed out of the kitchen

"Where do you think you're going? We're not done here!"

"We're beyond done!"

"Silke," Dad's voice, incredibly, was calm.

But I was too tightly wound now. He wanted to help me and Mom make peace, but I didn't trust him anymore, either. "Shut up! You're nothing but a lying cheat!"

I heard Mom gasp.

"Hey!" Dad bellowed. I had never heard him sound like that. It scared me. But things were already in motion; it was too late now.

I shifted from a quick walk to a sprint, and was out the front door and down the block before I realized I didn't have my shoes on.

CHAPTER SIXTEEN

I kept running. I didn't hear anyone behind me, but I wasn't going to take any chances. I ran between houses, turned at almost every corner I came to, and ran even though it felt like someone had shoved a knife between my ribs.

I hadn't been afraid before, but I was now. I didn't know what to do or where to go. The only thing I knew, the only absolute, was that I couldn't go home. It was crazy—it was stupid—how fast everything had blown up. I knew it. I knew I had overreacted. But it had to be done. I couldn't keep going, keep being shoved into that mold of complete submission anymore. As cheesy as it sounded, I had to be me.

Slowing down because I simply couldn't run any more, I started to look around at where I had actually gone. I was nearly downtown. Sudden, violent shivers hit me. I didn't have a jacket, either.

I had to go somewhere. I didn't have my purse, or any cash. I didn't even have my cell phone. By now, I was sure my parents would have called all my friends, so I couldn't go to their houses anyway. I really had no choice but to go home, but I was desperate to come up with something else to do.

A hand came down on my shoulder, and I jumped and screamed and started to run all at once.

"Silke!"

I stopped short and tried to turn around too fast, stumbling. Dominic reached out a hand and steadied me.

"Wow, you should play basketball," Dominic rumbled. His hair was pulled back in his dark ponytail.

"What?"

"You can jump really, really high."

"Shut up," I snapped. "What are you doing?"

"Just out for a walk."

"Here?"

"Here I am."

"Why?"

"Why not?"

I ground my teeth to stop from yelling at him.

"Where are you going?" he asked.

"I don't know."

"Where were you?"

"In hell."

He blinked. "Really?"

I waved him off. "Never mind."

He grinned, his teeth flashing. "You're mad at me."

"No."

He stopped smiling. "No?"

"Do you want me to be mad at you?"

"I don't know," he shrugged. "You're kind of cute when you're mad."

"That's stupid."

He shrugged again. "You're cold," he observed.

"No," I said, shivering more than I wanted to.

"Go home," he advised. "I bet it's warm inside."

"Where are you going?" I asked as he turned to walk away.

"Out."

"Why?"

"No reason."

"Want to order a pizza?"

"Just order it? Or eat it too?"

"Never mind," I said in disgust, turning away.

"I'm sorry," he said. "I don't know why I keep doing that."

"Doing what?"

"Being a jerk when you're being nice."

"Maybe because you're a jerk," I said.

"Ah," he said as he fell in step with me, "There are the claws. I knew you had some."

I was walking fast because I wanted to warm up. My feet

had passed from numb to a slight burning sensation because they were so cold.

"So where are you going in such a hurry?" he asked.

"Anywhere else."

"Want to come with me?"

"We're already here. I'm going someplace else."

"Yeah, well, I've changed my mind. Instead of going out, I'm going to go home and order a pizza. Want to come?"

"Yes, please," I said, nearly crying with relief.

"Uh, Silke?"

"What?"

"You don't have any shoes on."

"I kn-n-n-ow," I chattered.

Dominic swore and in one swift motion took his flannel shirt and wrapped it around my shoulders. He left his arm there, too, and pulled me close to his side.

"You'll f-f-f-freeze," I protested.

"And you're already frozen," he said. "Come on, let's get you inside."

*   *   *

I wasn't really aware of how we got to Dominic's. I was so cold and my feet hurt so bad that all I could do was watch where I put them, one after the other, trying to avoid big rocks and broken glass. I don't think we walked very far, but I was in a neighborhood I didn't recognize and I was in serious pain. I know it didn't take long, but it felt like hours. It did register that he lived in an apartment, all the way up on the fifth floor.

Inside, Dominic steered me to a couch. As he took his arm off my shoulder, I dropped onto the cushion, and Dominic disappeared for a moment but quickly returned and draped a blanket over me.

I closed my eyes and when I opened them again, there was a steaming mug on the coffee table in front of me. Something pulled on my foot again, and I realized that was what had woken me. Dominic was tugging the remainder of my socks off my feet.

"Hsssttt," I sucked in my breath. His warm hands felt like fire on my cold skin.

He let out a low whistle. "I don't know how you're going to walk on these tomorrow," he said. "You're cut up pretty bad."

"I'll be all right," I said. It was strange how his gentle hands on my feet could make my stomach tingle.

He picked up a washcloth and began wiping my feet. The tingle in my stomach vanished as my feet howled in pain. I tried not to whimper.

"What were you thinking?"

"I wasn't."

"What happened?"

But I was staring at his head. He looked up at me. "Silke?"

"Take out your ponytail." Outside, in the dark, it had looked like the natural brown of his hair. In the living room light, however, it wasn't dark brown; it was black. There wasn't a hint of a stray blue or red strand; the white tips were gone. Every hair on his head was as black as shoe polish.

He looked back down at my feet. "Tell me what happened to send you running without shoes."

"No—you tell me. What are you wearing? What am I wearing?" The flannel shirt he had wrapped over my shoulders was a solid black, not the normal plaid he usually wore. The t-shirt that stretched across his back as he tended to my feet was black, too. "Dominic," I reached forward and grabbed his hands, pulling them up toward me, pulling him toward me. "Dominic, what happened?"

He looked up at me, silent tears rolling down his face. He gave me a sad smile, and shrugged.

"Oh, Dominic!" I slid from the couch to the floor, and wrapped my arms around him.

He put his head on my shoulder and simply rested there. Once in a while he trembled, and I knew it wasn't because he was cold. We were quiet for a while. I didn't know what to say, but I got the feeling that I didn't need to say anything.

"This morning," he said, answering my thoughts. "They called me on the way to school. She was going fast." He paused for a few seconds. I squeezed his shoulders a little more. "She couldn't talk by the time I got there. But…but I think….*hope* that …that she knew…I was there." He was trembling again. I stroked his back, smoothing his shirt down his spine.

"She knew," I whispered to him. "She knew you were there."

He sniffed. "I don't—"

"She knew," I insisted. "Your presence fills the room as soon as you walk in."

"We talked about you yesterday, when I went back. She liked you, Silke," he said. "She said you were good for me." He paused again. "You were the last person she met."

My tears came then. We held each other in the silence of the apartment, and time passed.

*   *   *

We didn't order a pizza. Neither of us were hungry.

"We can order a pizza tomorrow," I said, finally feeling cozy and sleepy in the corner of his couch.

"Dad'll be here at ten," he said. "He wants us gone by noon."

I choked on the cool tea I was drinking. "Seriously?"

"Plane tickets are already bought."

"He's that much of an ass?"

"My dad's a good guy," Dominic said with a sigh. "I know I've kinda made him sound bad, but really, the only bad thing about him is that he wanted me to move out there before Mom…before she…" he stopped and cleared his throat. "I couldn't leave her here alone, you know? I'm the only family she has…had. I wanted to be here; he wanted me there so I could start at the beginning of the school year. He thought it'd be easier on me, and easier on her, too. She wouldn't have to worry about me, he said. He said he'd fly me back before she got...you know, really bad. But she already was."

"He didn't know that?"

"The doctors didn't know it. But she knew it. And I knew it, cause it showed in her eyes."

I nodded. Her eyes had been bright yesterday, but not in the right way.

"So where were you going?" I asked.

"Huh?"

"When you found me, lost and wandering the dark streets alone," I intoned dramatically, "Where were you going?"

"Oh, to the shop," he said. "There are a couple things I want to get, and I'm not sure I'll have time to stop by in the morning."

"So let's go."

He blinked. "We can't go now."

"Why not?"

"You shredded your feet."

"They're fine," I said, even though they hadn't stopped throbbing. He still hesitated, clearly not believing me. "I'm not going to be the reason you didn't go to your mom's shop one more time," I said.

"Hang on," he said. He disappeared into one of the bedrooms. I leaned over and looked at my feet. My left one looked worse than my right one, even though it was my right one that hurt more. Walking was going to hurt for several days, but I wasn't going to let Dominic know it tonight.

"Here," he said, coming back with a pair of socks and moccasin style slippers. "They'll be big, but at least they'll give you a little cushion."

"I don't want to tear up your slippers," I said.

"The shop's just a block away," he said. "You won't hurt them too much."

"You were taking the long way to the shop, huh?"

"Yeah," he said. "I did some wandering of my own. I needed

to walk."

"I'm glad you did."

"Me too." He handed me a faded denim jacket.

As we walked to the shop, even holding hands with Dominic wasn't enough to block out the pain from my feet. So I asked, "When's your Mom's funeral?"

"She didn't want one," he said. "She's going to be cremated, and then I'm supposed to go scatter her ashes."

"Where?"

"I don't know. She said she left a letter with instructions in it with Dad. I'm not supposed to scatter them for a while, though. She said something about sending me on a special trip when I graduate high school or something. She was kind of flighty."

"Free spirited," I corrected.

He looked at me and grinned. "Yeah. You got that just from yesterday, huh?"

I shrugged.

"She said she liked you because you could see through my front; I don't think she knew you saw right through hers, too."

"I only know she's free spirited because of you."

"What do you mean?"

"Look at you. She let you be whoever you want to be."

"I didn't give her much of a choice."

I laughed. "That I can believe."

*   *   *

It didn't take Dominic long to gather the things he wanted from the shop: her cosmetology certificate, her "silver scissors" and matching comb, and a couple of pictures of the two of them. Still, when he finished, he sat on one of the chairs and looked around.

I sat in the other chair, and looked at pictures of various models and hairstyles that were taped to the walls above the mirrors. Almost all of them had bright colors and radical cuts.

My eyes dropped to the mirror in front of me, taking in my white-blonde hair with the new bangs and layers.

The boring style that had upset my mom.

"D'ya still like it?"

I met Dominic's eyes in the mirror. He looked so unsure.

"I love it," I said, "But it's missing something."

"Oh?"

"I think it needs some color."

He grinned. "Are you gonna show your real personality? Become a red-head to go with that fiery temper of yours?"

"I don't think I want to go all red," I said.

"Well you can't go rainbow," he said flatly. "I own that look."

"You gave it up," I said, nodding toward him. "You look like a vampire with that black hair and clothes."

He jumped out of the chair and got right behind me. "I *am* a vampire, and I'm here to suck your blood!" He leaned down so we were cheek to cheek, staring at each other in the mirror, and then he pinched the sides of my neck.

To my mortification, I screeched.

He laughed and stood up, grabbing the ends of my hair and lifting it, letting it fall back to my shoulders. "So what are we going to do?"

Emerald eyes watched me, not judging, not demanding, not doing anything but watching me. And for some reason, I felt that he was the only one who really saw me. I wasn't good at creative things. Time lines and integers I understood; impressionism and symbols not so much.

"I trust you," I said.

"Sincerely?"

"Sincerely," I said, and I closed my eyes.

He spun the chair so I was facing him. I opened my eyes to find him leaning forward on the arms, almost forehead to forehead with me. "Nope," he said, shaking his head. "I love that you trust me, but you have to make your own decisions."

"Red," I said.

He raised his eyebrows.

"But not all red," I said slowly. He turned the chair so I was facing the mirror again. "Just one lock," I said. I reached up and took a small section of hair on the left side of my head. "Right here."

He took a comb and deftly parted my hair, sectioning off about an inch wide swath. "This?"

I nodded.

"Red?"

"Not red-red, not a fire engine," I said. "A soft red."

"Pink?"

"No," I said. "A pale magenta?" I offered.

Dominic frowned, considering. He nodded slowly. "I think we could do that. In fact, it'd probably be hard to get a dark color. I'm not sure how well your hair will hold any color. But you need more than just this." He pulled on the lock he was holding and then tilted his head. "Let's do stripes."

"No!" I yelped. "I'll look like a candy cane!"

He laughed. "I hadn't thought about that. Okay, I know what we're doing."

He disappeared in the back room, and the radio came on. A few moments later, he was back out with a plastic tub and assorted items in it. He opened a bottle and mixed some chemicals in it, then came to stand in front of me.

"*Now* you can close your eyes," he said.

I obliged.

"So, you still haven't told me what you're doing here."

"Getting my hair done," I murmured, "Then I thought you could give me a manicure."

"Funny girl," he said, tugging lightly on my hair.

"I had a fight with my parents."

"About the hats?"

"No. About the whole weekend."

"Oh. They found out, huh?" he said sympathetically. "What happened?"

"I don't even know," I said.

"Hey, you don't get off that easy."

"What do you mean?"

"Spill it," he ordered.

"There's nothing to spill," I said. "Mom freaked a little about my hair, she—" Dominic's gentle tug on my hair suddenly got harder, but I ignored him. "—freaked a little more when I told her I had stayed with Bridget instead of Alexi, and then she just completely lost it when she found Friday's pizza box in the trash."

"What was she doing in the trash?"

"Damned if I know," I said.

"Tell the truth, are you dying your hair to freak her out even more?"

I opened my eyes and met his worried ones. "No. I'm just tired of everything always being the same. I want different."

"You were different from the beginning," he said. "No one else was willing to talk to me. People think McNair is uptight, but man! Brevard's got snobbery all tied up."

"I want new for me," I said.

"Okay," he said, sectioning off part of my bangs.

"No candy cane," I pleaded.

"No candy cane," he agreed.

*   *   *

"I love it," I breathed. The left half of my bangs and the first section of long hair on my right were a soft pink with just a hint of lavender.

"It's not red," Dominic said, hovering behind me. He had begun to get worried about five minutes before he washed the color treatment out. "I'd call it fuchsia."

"I love it," I repeated. "It's much better than red."

"You sure?"

"Thank you so much!" I said, throwing my arms around him and hugging him. "It's perfect!"

"You're just saying that."

"Nope. I mean it."

We cleaned up together, then he said, "So, you ready to go home?"

I stopped. "I don't want to go home."

"It's late, Silke. You've got to go home."

"But—"

"Your parents have got to be really freaked out by now."

"Which is exactly why I don't want to go!"

"Silke," Dominic said in a patient rumble, "You know you have to go home."

"No," I said stubbornly, "I don't."

"Silk—"

"You can go to my house if you want to, but I'm not going."

"Where will you go?"

"I don't know," I said. "I'll go to a shelter if I have to."

"You're being ridiculous."

I crossed my arms and stood there, staring at him.

He sighed. "Fine. You win. I'm not going to leave you to wander the streets by yourself. You can come to my house, on one condition."

"What's that?"

"If you trusted me, you'd just say okay."

"You know I trust you," I said, "But not at this particular moment. What's the condition?"

"You have to call your parents."

"No."

"Silke, come on, you're being unreasonable!"

"They will be more upset if I tell them that I'm spending the night at your house than they would be if I said I was sleeping on a park bench."

"Then don't tell them where you are," he said. "Just tell them that you're okay."

I sighed. "Fine." I shivered. "Can we go now?"

Dominic handed me his cell.

"I'll call later."

He shook his head. "You'll call now."

"But—"

"Now, Silke."

When I hesitated, he took the phone from me again. I didn't have time to feel relieved, because he immediately began dialing the phone, and I knew exactly what number he was calling.

"You can talk to them," I said.

"Okay."

He held the phone up to his ear. I heard the first ring, and I ripped the phone out of his hand.

I intended to hang up the phone, but I heard Grete say, "Hello?" Her voice was so small.

"Hi, Grete, it's—"

"Silke!" she screamed. "Silke! Are you okay? I want—"

"Silke?" Mom's yell hurt my ear a lot more than Grete's scream had. "Where are you?"

"Tell Grete I'm fine, since she's the one who asked," I snapped. "That's why I called, to tell you I'm okay."

"You had better get your butt home—"

"I'm not coming home," I managed not to shout, though I really wanted to.

"Silke—" There was some shuffling and Mom's irate voice moved away.

"Silke, honey, are you okay?" Dad's voice suddenly filled my ear. "Silke?"

Suddenly I was on the verge of tears. I swallowed hard. "I'm fine. I'm not coming home right now, but I'm fine."

"Where are you?"

"I'm fine."

"When will you come home?"

I hesitated. "Maybe tomorrow."

"Maybe?" Dad asked while Dominic suddenly glared at me.

"I'll call tomorrow," I said more certainly, turning away from Dominic.

"Silke, please," I had never heard Dad beg before, and it almost hurt. "Where are you?"

"I'm with a very good friend," I said, looking up at Dominic. "And I'm fine."

I snapped the phone shut.

Almost immediately, it rang, my home number showing on the screen. I handed the phone to Dominic. "They'll be calling all night," I said.

He set the phone on the counter and then picked up the box of his mother's things. "It won't bother us."

At the door, he stopped and looked around one more time, hand on the light switch. His phone stopped ringing. I wondered what Mom and Dad would think when they heard Dominic's deep voice say, "Yo, too busy for you now. Leave a message for when I get bored."

I put my hand on his shoulder, but couldn't think of a thing to say.

He flipped the lights off, and as he pulled the door shut behind him, his phone started ringing again. Dominic locked the door. As we started walking, he said, "Thank you."

"For what?"

"That's probably the last time I'll ever do someone's hair."

I laughed. "You're good at it."

"If I were good, I would have gotten your color right."

"You did," I said, "It's exactly what I want."

"It's not what you asked for," he countered.

"That's only because I didn't know what to ask for."

CHAPTER SEVENTEEN

"Talk to me."

"Nothing to talk about."

"Silke—"

"Seriously, there's nothing to talk about."

"Some people might run away from home for no reason, but you're not one of them."

"I didn't run away from home!"

Dominic cocked an eyebrow at me.

"Okay, so I kind of ran away. And I know it's stupid, but I didn't have a reason."

"I'm going to kick you out."

"You wouldn't," I said, nestling comfortably back in the couch cushions. "But," I continued before he could say anything else, "I guess, if I had to pick a reason, it's that I'm tired of Mom being such a control freak."

"Really? You ran because you're Mom's acting like—"

"A Nazi," I muttered.

"—herself, not because your father rigged the hats?"

"Oh, I'm mad about that," I said, thinking of Dad's shocked face when I called him a lying cheat. "But what drove me out the door was Mom freaking because we had pizza on Friday."

"She knew I was there?"

"Oh, God, no! I can't imagine what she'd do if she found out that we spent the whole weekend at the house by ourselves. She'd probably drop d—" I stopped, horrified by what I almost said. "She'd ground me until I was thirty," I said instead.

"So you're not going to tell her when you go home tomorrow?"

"I'm not suicidal yet."

"Hello!"

I jumped, spilling my cold tea on the couch.

"You didn't tell me you were having company," Ivy said, using her hip to shut the front door behind her. Dominic hopped up and took one of the grocery bags from her and carried it to the kitchen.

"Sorry," he said, "I didn't think she'd interfere with our plans too much."

"You have plans?" I asked, trying to mop up the couch with the bottom of my shirt.

"We're having a wake," Ivy said.

"Oh."

Dominic tossed me a dishtowel. "We're just going through some boxes of photos Mom's collected over the years."

"Lori could've been a professional photographer," Ivy said, shaking her head. "Why she wanted to waste her life doing hair, I'll never know."

"But aren't—" I stopped, realizing I was about to put my foot in my mouth again.

"But that means you're wasting your life," Dominic said, finishing my thought for me, "So why couldn't she, since it made her happy?"

Ivy smacked him lightly on the shoulder. "*I'm* not wasting my life. I've always enjoyed working with people and making them pretty. Plus, I wasn't good at anything else. Lori was good at whatever she tried." Ivy put her arm around Dominic and leaned her head against his. "Like you." She kissed him on the forehead and then stepped away. "First things first," she said briskly, clapping her hands. "Food."

"No thanks," Dominic said.

I said, "Neither of us are very hungry."

"Kids without appetite aren't healthy. You need to eat."

Thirty minutes later, we were sitting around a small kitchen table with sliced cheese, meat, fruit, and crackers in the middle, with four shoeboxes placed in front of the empty chair. Ivy poured us each a glass of wine, after extracting the promise that we weren't leaving the apartment tonight and that we wouldn't tell anyone she let us drink.

Dominic handed us each a box. "We're looking for the good ones," he said.

"I'm telling you they're all good," Ivy said. "You're not going to be able to get rid of any of them. Just pack the boxes already."

Dominic shook his head. "I don't want all of them. Just the good ones. Then I can scan them and don't have to keep all the prints."

Ivy shook her head in return and muttered something that sounded like "You're going to want to keep them all!"

It felt weird, looking through someone else's photos. Ivy was right; Lori was talented. My box had a lot of photos of flowers and birds, most of them good enough to be in a professional calendar. There were duplicates, which Dominic decreed would go in one pile. There were also a very few that were a little out of focus; I guessed that they had been taken before she got into digital pictures.

The photos didn't seem to have any chronological order to them. I'd find a picture of Dominic when he looked to be five, then a picture of Lori at her high school graduation, followed by a picture of Dominic in a high chair.

"Oh, look how cute you were!" Ivy sighed, and held up a photo of Dominic, probably three or four years old, sitting next to Lori and holding a stuffed tiger while they looked out at a snowstorm. "Can I keep it?"

"If there's a duplicate," he said, looking at it for a moment. "I think that was the Christmas before the divorce. Dad took that one."

A few minutes later, he was laughing so hard he couldn't tell us what was funny.

"Let us see," Ivy demanded.

He shook his head, holding the photo out of her reach, which put it right in front of me.

I burst out laughing and pulled it out of his hand at the same time.

"Hey, hey, give it back!" he gasped.

I handed it to Ivy. It showed Dominic, about two years old, wearing nothing but diapers and sunglasses, which would have been funny enough, but he also had struck the disco pose, one hand pointing up and the other down. He even had his hip out.

It took us nearly ten minutes to stop laughing about that photo, and for the rest of the evening, all it took was one snicker to get all three of us howling with laughter.

In between looking at photos, Dominic and Ivy reminisced about Lori. Several times they teared up, but almost right away they found something funny to laugh about. It occurred to me, as we finished dividing the photos, that I had attended my first funeral.

Dominic ended up with three boxes of photos, which meant both of them claimed victory. Ivy said she was right because he hadn't gotten rid of any photos; Dominic said he was right because by giving all the duplicates to Ivy, he had condensed the photos into three boxes instead of four. There weren't more than two-dozen fuzzy photos, and at the end, Dominic slipped them into one of the boxes with a sheepish look on his face. But neither Ivy nor I said anything. We understood why he wanted to keep them.

"Who's ready for movies and dessert?" Ivy asked after she stashed her box of photos in her room.

"Whatcha got in mind?" Dominic asked.

"Only the best for my nephew's last night under my roof," she said.

"Really?"

She smiled and stepped into the kitchen. "Find something worth watching," she said. "Dessert'll be out in ten."

"Can I help?" I asked, feeling awkward.

"Go help him," she said, nodding to where Dominic was kneeling in front of a shelf of DVDs. "It's all about him tonight."

I nodded and joined Dominic in front of the shelf.

"Ivy makes the best key lime pie," he said. "I know it's out of a box, but she does *some*thing to it. I use the same brand of stuff, and it sucks. I've tried to get her to tell me what she adds, but she won't."

"So what qualifies as something worth watching?" I asked, scanning the eclectic collection of titles.

"Tonight, it's got to be one of Mom's favorites," he said. "But it's also got to be something I can stand to watch."

"*Pride and Prejudice* is always good," Ivy called from the kitchen.

Dominic made retching noises.

"*Saturday Night Fever*?" I suggested, causing all of us to go in hysterics again.

"I'm going to blow the disco baby photo of you up to a poster," Ivy called, "And I'm hanging it in the living room above the TV."

"I kept that one."

"It had a duplicate."

"No it didn't!" But Dominic shot me a look of pure panic. "Did it?" He whispered to me.

"I have no idea," I whispered back.

He swore. "She'd do it, too, just to torture me," he said quietly. Louder, he said, "How about *Transformers*?"

"Come on, Dom."

"Well, I don't want to watch something that makes you cry," he replied.

"I like that plan."

In the end, he chose *Pirates of the Caribbean*. "She always wanted to take a vacation there," he said, "And it's got a bit of a love story to it."

"Yeah, but at the end they can only be together one day every ten years," I said.

He shrugged. "She'd tell you waiting is worth it for true love."

"Did she wait for your dad?"

"No," he said shortly, "Which is why she is...was...became a big believer in waiting."

"Oh."

The key lime pie was fantastic, and the movie kept us all entertained, though I did catch Dominic staring off at the wall from time to time.

Clean up was quick, because the three of us polished off the whole pie. Ivy disappeared in her room for a moment, and came back with a pillow and blanket.

"So who's on the couch tonight?"

"I am," we both said at the same time.

"No," Ivy said, "You're not sleeping on the couch together."

"I'll take it," I said quickly, "It makes more sense—you don't have to change sheets on the bed."

"Who said I was going to change the sheets?" Dominic asked.

"My room is the one in between Dominic's room and the living room," Ivy said, "And I'm a very light sleeper, so I will know if either of you get up to change locations."

My face was bright red. Dominic was merely rolling his eyes.

"I'm serious, Dom," she said.

"You think you are," he said, "And that's what makes it funny."

*   *   *

Less than an hour after Ivy checked on both of us and declared lights out, Dominic came into the living room with a blanket. He spread it out on the floor in front of the couch.

When I asked him what Ivy was going to do when she caught him, he laughed. "She has three alarm clocks and still oversleeps for work sometimes. She's not going to catch us."

"So what are you going to say to your parents tomorrow?" he asked.

"Still haven't thought about it," I said.

"Well, I've got a plan for you."

"Really?"

"Yep. Tell 'em everything. Come clean. Honesty is the best

policy."

I snorted. "Yeah, right."

"Sincerely. It's the same thing as ripping the Band-Aid off. Do it fast and get it all over with. If you only tell them part, you're going to be worried and miserable about getting found out about the rest of it. And when you do get caught, they'll be even angrier, and they won't believe you when you say there's nothing else."

"Okay, when you say it like that, it sounds simple and logical. But doing it...."

"You've got to, Silke. It's really your only option."

"What if I just really run away? Ivy's gonna have a spare room tomorrow. I could work for her."

"You'd really be wasting your talents if you went the cosmetology route," he said. "And Ivy's not fun to live with. Tonight has been a very exceptional exception."

"So I'll join a circus."

"I didn't do *that* bad of a job on your hair."

"Umm—" I was running out of ideas.

"Okay, consider this. If you run away, the chances of me seeing you again are very small."

"If I tell my parents about you spending the night—"

"They freak," he said simply. "And you tell them nothing happened. And you tell them again, and again. And you and I will send emails. And write letters. And I will call and I will be polite on the phone. And we'll both be on the honor roll."

"Still not going to be enough."

"And we play the pity card: my mom was dying and you were the only ray of light in my life."

That just might work, I thought later as we dozed off. In my dreams, anyway, it did.

*   *   *

I slept well, but not long. It was still dark when my eyes popped open. There was a triangle of light spilling out of the room at the end of the hall, so I could see that Dominic and his makeshift bed were gone.

Quietly I padded to his room. Outside the door I stopped, torn. Should I knock and run the risk of waking Ivy, or should I just walk in, possibly while he was changing clothes? I settled for tapping my fingernails lightly against his door.

I had to do it twice, but finally he swung the door open.

"What are you doing up?" he whispered. "It's not even five yet."

"Couldn't sleep. Why are you up?"

"Same." He shut the door behind me without making a sound.

"You got a lot done," I whispered. His room was all boxes. Nothing hung on the wall or took space on top of the dresser. The mattress was bare; a pile of blankets topped by a pillow sat at the foot of the bed.

"I've been packing all week," he said. "I knew I wasn't going to be able to put Dad off much longer, not matter what I did. My next excuse was going to be mono. His wife would insist I stay away for at least three weeks after getting a clean bill of health from a doctor."

"He's going to be here at ten?"

"Yep. Flight gets in at eight, he'll pick up the U-Haul, we'll load it up, and be on the road by noon."

"Not much time for good-bye."

"Not many to say good-bye too."

I nodded, looking down at my hands.

"Hey," he said softly, nudging me with his foot, "You know I'm not saying good-bye to you, right?"

"Just gonna leave me hanging?"

He sighed and said patiently, "I mean it won't be good-bye."

I smiled, but my tears blurred his face. "I think it has to be. But—it sounds cheesy—but there's this thing that I've seen on-line before. I can't remember exactly how it goes, but it's something like: some people come into your life for a day or a year, and some leave footprints for a lifetime. I think you're a footprint."

"Well yeah," he said, "But that's just because you let me walk all over you." He nudged me again with his foot. "The one Mom always talked about was that people come into your life for a reason, a season, or a lifetime."

"I've seen that one too," I said.

"I think they both work. You know that you screwed everything up for me, right?"

"I what?"

"I had it all set. I said good-bye to everyone at McNair last year. This year, at a new school, no one knew me, I wasn't going to get to know anyone, I could come in, go out, move on, no problem. And then there was you."

"You didn't have to talk to me."

"Yeah I did."

"You could have asked someone else—"

"Norton gave me the excuse to talk to you. But I knew I was going to talk to you from the moment I walked in that class. You were the only one who actually looked me in the eye. Everyone else just saw what I wanted them to see, my hair. But not you. You actually looked at *me*. We're connected, Silke. And it's an elastic cord. It can stretch between wherever we are, if you let it."

*   *   *

I didn't stick around to meet his dad. Dominic asked me to, but I just couldn't. I was going to be a blubbering mess, and I didn't need leave that as a first impression. I tried to leave around eight, but I got sidetracked.

First, Dominic wouldn't let me leave the apartment without shoes, and I wouldn't take his fur-line leather slippers. He insisted on waking Ivy to ask her for a pair of shoes.

She gladly gave me a pair of flip-flops. I told her I'd bring them back, but she waved that off.

"I don't care about the shoes, but you'd better come visit me at the shop. I don't want you letting anyone else touching up that radical hair."

Before I could reply, Dominic said, "And don't let anyone else talk you out of it, either. If you get tired of it, fine. But if you really do *love it*!" He squealed in fair imitation of my response last night, "Then you won't care what other people say."

"Getting rid of it is not an option," I said firmly, "Adding some emerald for contrast, now that I might talk about."

"Then you definitely have to come see me," Ivy said, and I could tell she didn't realize I was joking. "I've got the perfect green. Next to that magenta, it'll clash with class."

"Okay, I'll come see you," I said, earning a crushing hug from her.

"Great. Now. Hum. I need...I gotta...I'll see you around!" Ivy said, and she trotted back to her room.

Dominic was shaking his head. "She's gonna lose it when I leave," he said. "It's not gonna be pretty."

"Should I come back this afternoon? To, like, check on her?"

"She'll probably go out," he said. "She'll be a mess, but that's kinda normal for her."

"So, now that I've got shoes on my feet, I think it's time to go."

Tilting his head to one side, Dominic said, "It hasn't warmed up that much. You need a jacket."

"I'll be fine," I said, not bothering to point out that my naked toes were going to get colder than my arms.

"Here," he said, grabbing the beat-up denim jacket he had leant me last night. It had a rip on the left sleeve and was missing the bottom button. "I was just gonna trash this anyway."

"Yeah?"

"Yeah."

He helped my put it on, and I felt a lot warmer. And safer. It smelled like him, clean and pepperminty, with a hint of hair chemical.

"Now you know there's one more obligation you have," he said with a grin.

"Oh? Another IOU?"

"Yep. Starts with an M."

I looked at him blankly. "I have no idea."

"Or I guess it could be a V."

"That didn't help at all."

"You've got to finish the *merry*-go-round. You know, go be a good *vandal*."

"Ah. Huh. Well, I'm not sure about that."

"It doesn't have to be right away," he said earnestly, "But it needs to be done. Sincerely. You don't leave a job like that unfinished. Get a friend to help you."

"You are so.....you." I wondered, though, what Alexi would say, what she would do, if I showed up late at night with a can of spray paint.

He grinned again. "Thank you. Now, obviously I don't have a new number yet," he said. "But I wrote your number down, so I'll call you. Just be sure you get your phone back by then end of the month, okay? I don't think I'll make it much longer than that."

"Okay."

"When are you going to call home?"

"Later."

"Silke—"

"Well, I'm not going to do it now," I said, exasperated. "They're at work, anyway."

He frowned at me. "You know better than that."

"I will call them today," I said. "That's all I promised, and I will keep my promise."

"Okay, so you'll call them to-*day*, before to-*night*."

I rolled my eyes. "Yes. Can I go now?"

"Do you have to?" His green eyes were so intense. How could I ever see anyone else's eyes attractive? "I know. You do. You're leaving, and I'm leaving, but we're not saying good-bye."

"Right," I said, opening the front door. I turned and looked at him, suddenly lost. I couldn't say good-bye, but really, what else was there to say?

S.L. ROTTMAN

CHAPTER EIGHTTEEN

I walked along Riverside with my arms wrapped around me, holding the jacket closed. I was trying to hold on to the feel of the hug Dominic had given me when I left; the sense of completion, the belief that we would see each other again, the realization that in just two short weeks, he had become an integral part of my life.

My feet kept moving because there wasn't anything else to do. They hurt, but it was a remote pain. My heart hurt so much more. I didn't start with a direction or goal in mind; for the moment it was more important for me to know where I wasn't going.

I wasn't going to wait around and meet Dominic's dad only to watch him take Dominic away from me.

I wasn't going home to wait for my parents to punish me.

I wasn't going to wait to let other people affect my life.

After walking for fifteen minutes or so, I knew where I wanted to go. Back to the bowling alley.

But less than a block away, I realized that the bowling alley, as fun as it had been with Dominic, wasn't going to do me any good today. For one thing, obviously, Dominic wasn't with me. Secondly, I didn't have any money.

It was time to get past what I wanted. It was time to focus on what I needed. I needed to talk to my parents. I needed the courage to say everything I'd been holding back for practically my whole life. I needed them to listen to me. I was afraid that if I went home, I'd lose what little nerve I'd gained.

"The library!" I was so excited by the idea I said it out loud as soon as I thought it. The library would be neutral ground, and it required quiet—Mom and Dad couldn't yell at me. We could actually sit and talk. Maybe. Hopefully.

I changed direction and headed to the public library.

As I walked, I tried to think about the conversation I needed to have. I couldn't tell Mom and Dad about Dominic spending the night, I decided, not so much because they would absolutely flip out, but because it was too precious. I imagined how the conversation would go again and again.

Mom would completely freak. She probably wouldn't let me finish the whole story before making appointments to get me checked out for STDs and checked into a home for unwed mothers. Dad would be crushed, once he accepted that I wasn't just joking around. Just thinking about his disappointment was enough to reduce me to tears. Even in the best scenario I could come up with, they were hurt, angry, and disbelieving. As innocent as Dominic and I had been, I just couldn't let their first impression of him be so wrong. He deserved better.

It would be hard to keep him to myself, but I thought I had to. I hadn't changed because of Dominic, but there was no way they would believe that. They would blame him for me becoming the new me, for me finally standing up for myself and claiming my rights.

I hadn't been to the library for a couple of years, Grete having outgrown the preschool story hour we used to take her to. But the soft sounds of people clicking on computer keys, the rustling of people looking through bookshelves, and the quiet conversations were appealing.

The teen room was located in the very back of the library. I walked past the children's section. A librarian I recognized was reading to a group of toddlers seated on the floor at her feet. The familiar scene was comforting.

There was a new couch, the old armchairs were gone and the old "READ" posters in the teen room had been replaced with new ones featuring different celebrities, but otherwise, it looked the same. I approached the desk cautiously. When a new librarian, or at least one I didn't remember, came around the corner, I was relieved. If it had been Mrs. Knesel, the librarian who ran all the teen activities, I would have been a lost cause.

"May I help you?" She was nice enough, but she arched her eyebrow at me, and I felt the need to explain.

"Yes, I'm here to do a little research for a project I'm doing. I'm home-schooled," I added, trying to make it sound like an afterthought instead of a lie. "How many pages am I allowed to print out?"

"As many as you want. They're fifteen cents each."

"Oh. Um, I didn't bring any money," I said.

She stared at me for a moment, then reached under the desk and pulled out a couple sheets of paper. "If you don't mind printing on the back of old flyers...."

"Oh, great!" I said. "Thank you! Can I borrow a pen, too?" She nodded.

I took the papers with me and found a table in the back. Because I had said I was doing research, I grabbed a few large science books off a shelf and spread them in front of me, opening two of them to random pages.

And then I set to work.

It took me almost an hour to get it all just right, and when I looked at it, it was hard to understand why it was so hard to do. But getting everything in the simplest form and in the right order wasn't easy. I recopied it and then realized I had left out a couple things, so I had to recopy it again.

I returned the books and threw away the first drafts, and then went back to the desk.

"Get everything you needed?" the librarian asked.

"Yes, thank you. Here's your pen," I added, setting it on the desk.

She smiled and turned back to the computer she was working on.

"Um," I squeezed my hands together, "Could I make a quick call?"

"Please take your cell phone outside," she said.

"Um, no, I meant, can I use this phone to make a quick call?"

Her eyebrows went up.

I tried to look guilty, which wasn't very hard, given how I was feeling. "My parents took my phone because I didn't finish the project on time."

"Ah. Please be quick," she said, nodding toward the phone.

My hand was shaking as I dialed my house number. I had told Dominic that my parents would be at work, and I desperately hoped they would be, but I knew that he was right. Of course they'd be home, and they'd be mad with worry.

"Hello? Silke?" Dad hadn't even let the phone finish ringing once. "Silke, is that you?"

"Hi, Dad," I said, feeling tears rush in. "I'm at the library."

"The library? I'm coming to get you—"

"No," I said, "I mean, yes, I want you to come, but bring Mom too, please. I'm in the teen room."

"Meet us at the front—"

"No," I said again, "Please meet me in the teen room."

"Silke—"

"I want—need to be able to talk to you and Mom, and I need to know that you'll listen. I'm in the teen room," I repeated in a weak whisper, fighting against the sobs that were threatening. I hung up the phone. "Thank you," I managed to strangle out to the librarian.

"Everything okay?"

I couldn't answer. I kind of shrugged and then hurried to the bathroom, where I locked myself in a stall and spent ten minutes sobbing, trying not to make a sound. The cold water in the sink did little to cover the fact that I had been crying, but it was the best I could do. And I had to be in the teen room before Mom and Dad got there. I didn't want to witness the scene that might play out if they didn't see me as soon as they walked in.

The teen room was even emptier than it had been when I left; the librarian wasn't behind the desk. Once again I went to the far back table. I sat down and put my hands in the jacket pocket, and my right hand found paper. I pulled out a small envelope with my name written across the front in familiar handwriting. I stuffed it back in the pocket immediately because just looking at Dominic's handwriting brought tears back. And then my parents came in, clinging to each other, clearly in a rush and looking panicky. My heart twisted.

When Dad saw me, he dropped Mom's arm and ran toward me, in violation of library rules everywhere. I stood up so he didn't have to yank me out of the chair.

He hugged me hard, then set me away from him and took my face in his hands. He stared at me. "You have no idea—" Dad finally let go of me and stepped back. "*I* have no idea what I'm feeling right now."

"I know exactly how I feel," Mom said before she also wrapped me in a hug. "So furious." She smoothed my hair down. "And so happy you're okay." She took a deep breath and then set me back. "Now. Let's get you home."

I ducked out of the arm she had around my shoulders. "No. We need to talk."

"We most certainly do," Mom said, and her voice was almost as imperious as it normally was. "That's why we're going home."

"We need to talk right here," I said, sitting down. My stomach felt like it was in my throat.

"Here? Why?" Dad asked.

"Maybe being in a public place will make all of us actually listen to each other and talk without shouting."

"I think it's more likely we'll get thrown out," Mom snapped. "Now let's go!" Her voice rose dangerously.

Dad looked at her for a moment, then said, "I think I understand where Silke's coming from," and he sat down across from me.

Mom stared at him in disbelief for a few seconds, and she looked so mad that I wasn't sure she was going to sit down. I really thought she might walk out on us.

Then she took a deep breath and sat down next to Dad. "Okay. A calm discussion about—"

"What I need," I said, pulling out my page. It already looked old and beaten, because I had been folding, unfolding, and refolding it so much. I flattened it out. "These are my needs."

"Your needs?" Mom said.

"Suddenly I feel like we're at a negotiation instead of a discussion," Dad said.

I ignored them both and began reading. "Number one: I need to be trusted."

"Of course," Dad said in surprise.

"You are," Mom said, "Or you were until this little incident."

"I need to be trusted *now*," I said. "As we talk about the last week and for the rest of my life, I need to be trusted."

"You must be trustworthy to be trusted," Mom said.

Dad put his hand over hers. "She is trustworthy, Teresa. She's not Lizzie. We've raised her well, taught her right from wrong, and she is not your sister. She's our daughter."

Mom clamped her mouth shut, and Dad nodded at me.

I continued, "Two: I need to be heard."

"That's why we're here."

"We're listening," Dad agreed.

"Three: I need to be believed."

"Okay."

"Didn't we agree to that when we said we'd trust you?" Mom asked. I looked at her. "Okay, we'll believe you."

"I need to be accepted for who I am, for my strengths and my weaknesses."

"Okay," they said together.

"Five: I need to be given permission to fail."

"What?" Dad said.

"No." Mom sat back and crossed her arms. "Absolutely not. I'm not going to tell you that you don't have to try."

"I'm asking that you trust me to try my best, believe me when I say I've tried my best, and recognize that I can't be perfect and get everything right every time. I have to be able to fail."

"I can recognize that you might fail, but I'm not going to give you permission to do it!"

Dad held up his hands. "Okay, we're getting bogged down in semantics on this one. Can we come back to it?"

"No. I'm tired of being terrified every time something goes wrong," I said. My breath caught as I tried to hold back the tears. "I'm tired of having to study for hours after I bring home a test that is a ninety-two percent."

"I don't—"

"Science, last year. I messed up on the vocabulary section. They were the only points I missed."

"So clearly you needed to study some more—"

"I was punished for bringing home an A."

"It wasn't punishment—"

"I had to study instead of going to Mariel's sleep over."

We locked gazes. I had never been able to stare Mom down before. The tears kept leaking from my eyes, but I wasn't going to give in.

"Getting a low A is not the same as failing," Mom said finally. "I'm not giving you permission to fail."

"No," Dad said, "You're right, Silke. I didn't realize you thought our expectations were too high. If you're going to be trustworthy, and admit it if you don't give it your best, then we'll understand that when you do give your best, that's all we can ask for."

I closed my eyes in relief. "That's all I want."

"Teresa?"

I opened my eyes and watched Mom looking at Dad. "If you do your very best all the time, that's all we can ask for," she said slowly.

"I need to be able to express myself."

"You're not giving us a choice, are you? Making us come here and stare at you with your punk hair."

"It's not punk," I said, hearing my defensive tone and hating it. "It's just different from what you're used to."

"It's getting removed tomorrow."

"You'll have to shave my head."

"I have no problem with that."

"Mom, it's only hair! It will grow out and change. It's not like I've gotten a tattoo or a piercing. Yet," I couldn't help adding.

Mom yelped. "You will NOT—"

"I don't want to. But I like my hair like this." I reached up and smoothed down the magenta stripe along my cheek. "I want to pick my own styles. I want to be me."

Mom crossed her arms. "Are we done yet? Because if this isn't the last one, we're going to be here for days."

I glanced at my list. "Three more," I said, "And then we can talk about everything else."

"I don't think I can handle it."

"Okay," I said, carefully keeping my voice in control. "Then I guess we're done."

"Great, let's go."

"No," Dad said, before I could say that I wasn't going anywhere until I was done saying what I needed to say. "We are not. We've made progress, but we're not done. She can express herself as long as it's nothing offensive."

"I find that offensive," Mom said, flinging her arm in my general direction. "That hair is not natural."

"Neither is pretending your perfect," I snapped. "Perfection is not only unnatural, it's unattainable."

"Offensive," Dad said quickly, cutting off whatever Mom's response was going to be, "Will be defined as obscene or insulting. This hair style is merely creative."

Once again I waited while Mom and Dad stared at each other. This time it felt longer.

"Freedom of expression," she said flatly. "As it is allowed in the Bill of Rights."

"I need to be given reasonable responsibilities." They were both silent, so I added, "Like the ones I have now. But no more."

"Wait. You're not trying to get out of your chores?"

Dad's lips twisted, and I almost thought he was trying not to smile.

"No. I'm okay with what I've got now. But I don't want any more for a while. And I want an open discussion when the time comes for more."

"Reasonable responsibilities," Dad said with a nod, and this time I saw the smile flash across his face.

"Eight: I need to be given reasonable restrictions," I said, and my voice sounded small.

"Like not being able to express yourself if it's crude or obscene?" Dad asked.

"Yes."

"Then I think we've covered that. Last one?"

"Last one. I need to know," I took a deep quivering breath, "That even if I do something wrong, you will forgive me."

"I'm sure that you wouldn't ever do anything really horrible," Mom said.

"We will always love you, Silke," Dad added. "Loving someone means that you will forgive them."

"Okay," I said, putting the list in the middle of the table where we could all see it. "Now that the rules have been agreed upon, do you want to hear about my weekend?"

"Truthfully, I'm not sure," Mom said, eyeing my hair. "It might give me nightmares."

"I want to hear everything," Dad said firmly.

So I told them, starting with Friday afternoon and not being able to find Alexi. I hadn't planned to tell them about Dominic—I wanted desperately to keep him to myself—but as I had written down my needs, I had realized that if I needed to be trusted and heard, then I also needed to be truthful. I wasn't hiding anything from anyone anymore—and that included myself.

Neither of them said anything until I got to Saturday night, when Dominic fell asleep on the floor.

"Wait," Dad said, "You're telling me this boy spent the night in our house?" Mom had gone pale and was making some strange noises in the back of her throat.

"On the floor," I said again, "He fell asleep on the floor, I slept on the couch. Nothing happened. He never touched me. We've never even kissed," I added.

"But he spent the night in our house?"

"Nothing happened," I repeated. "So Sunday morning, Bridget called."

"And you spent the rest of the weekend with her?" Mom half-guessed, half-suggested.

It was so tempting, right then, to just say yes, that I had spent the rest of the weekend with Bridget. I had the feeling that Mom and Dad would rather believe me than call and check to make sure I was telling the truth. But I had promised—myself, them, and Dominic—that I would tell them the whole truth.

So I told them about the rest of Sunday, and showing Dominic the magic hats. I was watching Dad, waiting for him to react when I said the top hat had fallen over, spilling the slips all over the floor. He didn't seem concerned.

"Silke, honey," Mom said suddenly, "Do you think we could finish this at home?"

"We're almost done," Dad said, "Aren't we Silke? Silke?" He repeated when I didn't answer him right away.

I was staring at Mom. She was pale and twisting her wedding band around and around on her finger.

"OhmyGod," I breathed.

She was staring at me, tears sparkling in her eyes. I couldn't rat her out. But I had promised to be completely truthful.

Dad looked from me to Mom and back again. "What's going on? What did I miss?"

I shook my head. I had no idea what to do or say.

"I'm sorry," Mom said, "But I really think we ought to go home now."

"Somebody'd better—"

"How about I tell you about the rest of it, and we come back to the magic hats?"

"What?"

"I think that would be best," Mom said.

"What?" Dad said again. "What is going on?" For the first time since sitting down, it was his voice that rose dangerously.

Now it was Mom putting her hand over his, Mom trying to soothe. "Please?"

"It won't take long," I said.

Dad was scowling, but he gave me a curt nod.

So I told them about Sunday night and Monday, and by the time I was talking about visiting Lori in the hospital, they were both very sympathetic.

"Poor boy," Mom murmured.

"It sounds like you both really needed each other," Dad said.

"Exactly!" I couldn't believe how quickly he understood that.

By the time I finished explaining last night's events, Mom had gone through two or three tissues.

"You were being a good friend, Silke," Dad said. "Perhaps not being the greatest daughter, but certainly the greatest friend you could be last night."

I smiled. "He helped me, too," I said.

"So, what about the hats?"

"Please, Heinrich, can we go home to talk about this?"

"No," he said. "We started here, we're going to finish here. Tell me what was wrong with the hats, Silke."

I looked at Mom and she nodded.

"All of the slips in the top hat said the same thing."

For a moment, Dad just stared at me. Then he said, "I don't understand."

"They all said, 'Go to Vegas.'"

Even though Dad continued to stare at me, I could sense a shift in focus.

"But your mother didn't want to go to Vegas," he said slowly, "She was upset about leaving."

"We weren't supposed to draw so soon," she said suddenly. "Labor Day weekend is in two weeks. I was going to put the hats out on Thursday night. I'd already been talking to Janet

Amerman and –"

"Why?" he asked, pushing his chair away as he turned to look at her. "Why couldn't you just suggest we go to Vegas? Why did you have to cheat—" He broke off and looked at me. "You thought I did it. That's why you called me a lying cheat before you ran out!"

I nodded miserably.

"I thought it'd be more fun if it came from the hat," Mom said desperately. "You love the hats, and I didn't think you'd put the hats out again that soon."

"Why can't you just have fun, Teresa? Why does everything always have to be by the rules—actually, not *the* rules, but *your* rules? What is so damn wrong with being spontaneous and doing things just for fun?" He stood up. "How many times have you rigged it before?"

"Never, I swear! I promise—"

"How can I believe that? How can I trust *you*?"

And he left.

CHAPTER NINETEEN

At first Mom had stayed seated at the table, almost like she couldn't get up and move. Then, suddenly snapping out of her trance, she had jumped up and bolted after Dad, yelling his name. I had been mortified as I chased after her, but not enough to slow down to a walk, like I should have. Out of the corner of my eye, I saw Mrs. Knesel at the front desk, gaping at us. I was sure our whole family would be banned from the library for the rest of our lives.

I caught Mom on the stairs in front of the library entrance, but Dad was nowhere to be seen. She was sitting on the middle step, face in her hands, sobbing.

I had never seen my mother cry before. I was at a complete loss. I sat next to her with my arm around her shoulders, trying to ignore the stares as people walked by. Fortunately, only one lady looked like she was going to stop or say something, but when I shook my head, she kept walking.

After what felt like hours, Mom finally raised her head. She wiped her face, for the most part successfully removing the smeared mascara from directly under her eyes.

"Okay," she said. "We need to go home."

We were quiet at the bus stop and the ride and the short walk home. As we walked in the front door, Mom called, "Heinrich?" And no one answered.

"Please pick Grete up from school today; she was awfully upset last night," was the only thing Mom said to me before she went to her room.

I walked into my room, thinking that today was even worse than I had imagined it playing out — but in a completely different way. I closed the door behind me, more out of habit than fear of being interrupted, then stretched out on my bed and looked at the envelope Dominic had left me.

On the back flap, he had written: For the record, I wrote this on Monday and was going to drop it at your house tomorrow. His sense of honesty made me smile.

Inside, there were two sheets of paper. One was a short note.

> Silke,
> You changed my life because you said yes. I have no doubt we'll meet again, and connect just as quickly. You are my reason for another season and a lifetime
> of hope.
>   Sincerely,
>   Dominic

The other paper had a sketch of me, with my new haircut but without the new color. At the bottom it said, Sincerely your friend.

Putting the note back in the envelope, I tacked it to the bulletin board above my desk, and then tacked the sketch over it. I could see it everyday, and know the sincere words he had written were right behind it.

I hung my list of needs on the bulletin board too, next to the sketch. I needed to remember them, or I might forget the rights I had fought for. I had gotten so used to being run over that I knew it would be easy to fall back in the habit.

Picking up my cell phone, I wasn't surprised to find that I had eleven missed calls. I was sure that Alexi was at least three or four of them, and Mariel and Emma would each be one. I wanted to check and see if Dominic had called too, but first I dialed Dad's number. It rang three times and went to voice mail. I hung up, counted to twelve, and hit redial.

"I need time, Silke," he said as soon as he picked up, "Just like you."

"Okay," I said, "But I told you when I'd call back, so…."

He sighed, and I could hear faint tapping. He was tapping his fingers on the steering wheel or a table somewhere. "I'll be home for dinner tonight."

"Do you want anything special?"

"Ha. I probably won't taste what I eat, so basic is good."

"Got it."

"Silk?"

"Yeah?"

"How mad were you when you thought I had rigged the hats?"

"Extremely."

"Yeah," he said, sighing again. "That's what I thought."

"See you at six."

"Yes. I love you, Silke."

"Love you too, Dad."

*   *   *

I was torn between leaving Mom alone and checking to make sure she was all right. I decided I would make lunch, and then see if she wanted any.

I had just finished setting out the sandwich fixings when she walked into the kitchen.

"Need any help?"

"I've got it," I said.

"Want to split a diet cola?"

"Sure."

She filled our glasses with ice, poured the soda, and then took hers to sit at the kitchen table.

"I'm sure you think that I'm a terrible hypocrite," she said, staring directly at the glass she held between both hands. "Always telling you that you must be truthful to be trustworthy and then going and rigging the hat." She sighed and looked up at the ceiling, shaking her head. "I *still* can't believe I did it. But I did. And I have to accept the consequences. You say you're tired of all my rules….well, I'm tired too, but I'm also afraid. I was afraid of losing you and Grete like Lizzie, and now I'm afraid I've lost you because of my fear. I know I need to let go, but I'm afraid to—and I don't know how to let go anymore. So I rigged the hats. I wanted to let the magic let us all go. And all I did was spoil the magic. Probably forever."

"No, Mom," I said, setting our sandwiches on the table. "Not forever. Just for now. We'll have to find a way to be responsible and still let go. We'll get the magic back. Somehow."

$*$ $*$ $*$

Dinner was quiet. Or it would have been, except Grete was all wound up. She screamed when she saw me waiting for her just like always after school. Twice I had to ask her to let go of my hand, because she was squeezing so hard. And then she followed me all over the house until I finally sent her to her room to do homework.

Dad came in just as I began to set the table, which was good, because I was starting to wonder if he really was coming home, and if not, would it be better to set the table for three instead of four. Mom gave him a scared little smile as he walked toward her. He gave her the briefest of kisses on the cheek, and then left the kitchen, returning with Grete when I called her for dinner.

Grete chattered about hide-n-go-seek, indignant that Jilly had accused her of *peeking*. She chattered about her spelling test, bragging about the fact she got *all* of the words right, *including* the bonus word. She chattered about the new song they were learning in music, because the *boys* didn't want to sing it. She chattered about lunch, and how great it had been to have *strawberry* milk today instead of chocolate.

But finally, even Grete ran out of things to chatter about, and I think she figured out that something was wrong, given the wide-eyed stare she was giving everyone by the end of the meal. Mom kept shooting frightened looks in Dad's direction; I never saw Dad look in Mom's direction at all. Dinner was finished in silence.

"Do you have any homework, Grete?" Dad asked as he cleared the table.

"Nope."

"Then I've got a real treat for you," he said, "Come with me!" And he scooped her up over his shoulder and carried her from the kitchen.

I methodically put the leftovers away and loaded the dishwasher. Mom didn't move.

"Okay," Dad said as he came back in, "She's set up with the new Barbie movie, so we can talk."

Mom looked at me and said, "Silke, you can have extra computer time to—"

"Silke can stay," Dad said evenly. "We're still not through discussing her escapade. I need a beer. Want one?"

"Yes please," Mom said meekly.

"Can I have another diet Coke?"

"Sure," Dad said, surprising me.

When the drinks were set at the table in front of us, it was suddenly awkward again.

"So," Mom cleared her throat, "Silke, what do you think we should do?"

"I don't know," I said honestly. "I'm sorry I lied. I wasn't trying to do anything bad, though. I just wanted some time alone—"

"Doesn't sound like you were alone very much," Dad pointed out.

"That just kind of happened," I said, feeling my face flush. "I only meant to spend the weekend here, out of trouble, and not cause you any worry."

"Well, thank you for that," Dad said, "Because we did have a great time." Mom looked up at him in surprise, but he continued, "But the point remains that you lied, and that you had a friend at the house when we weren't home, which is breaking our rules, not to mention the fact that said friend spent the night and is male."

I nodded, because there didn't seem to be anything to say.

"You ran away from us instead of talking, though in retrospect, that did give all of us time to calm down, and it also let us know how serious this is to you. I think, if your mother agrees, that being under house arrest until Halloween is probably severe enough."

I was afraid to breathe. I had been hoping to get away with house arrest from now until New Year's, maybe, but really thought they'd ground me for at least six months.

Mom was gently spinning her beer glass between her hands. "I don't know," she said. "On the one hand, it doesn't seem like enough. On the other, it seems like too much." She looked up at me, and I snapped my mouth shut. "I think that perhaps I haven't been giving you the trust and freedom that you've earned over the years, though, as I said earlier, you have broken that trust with your actions this weekend."

"I'm sorry," I whispered.

"I'm sorry too," she said, and she smiled while tears reflected in her eyes. "Because although you'll only be grounded until Halloween, there's no way you're going on the choir trip to New York."

I nodded. It hurt, but I understood.

"Silke? Anything else to add?" Dad asked.

"I won't hide anything like this from you again," I said.

"How about you won't do anything like this again?" Mom countered immediately. "Because otherwise we ought to look at grounding you for the rest of the school year so you can really think about it."

"I won't do anything like this again," I said quickly, "And I'll talk to you when I feel too much pressure instead of just freaking out."

"I like that," Dad said, "I don't need any more freaking out."

"Me either," Mom said.

"Okay."

"Okay."

"Okay," Dad chimed in last. And then we just sat there, and it was awful and awkward all over again.

"Um—"

"Why, Teresa?" Dad burst out. "Why did you have to cheat just to have fun? Is it really so hard for you to say you want to do something fun and spontaneous?"

"Yes," she said, for the second time in one day I was watching my mother cry. "I don't know how to...to let go of ...to be free from...to....." she trailed off, shaking her head, and then she looked directly at me. "You think it's hard living in someone else's rules when you feel trapped? Try freeing yourself from rules you've made. It's even harder." She looked back at Dad. "It's so hard to find freedom."

"How often have you done this?"

"Never. This was the first time. You've always wanted to go to Vegas. Labor Day weekend is wide open, and I thought...."

"I love you for thinking it, but why? Why not just say 'Let's go away for Labor Day?' That's what I don't understand."

"I thought it was harmless. It wasn't going to hurt anyone, it was just a way to have fun and give you something you wanted. But in hindsight—it was a lie. And lying is wrong. No matter the reason."

"I don't think we can ever use the hat again."

They both looked at me, and I realized that the sudden, strange, high-pitched squeak had come from me.

"What?" Dad asked, sounding exasperated, "Don't pretend you've ever liked the hats."

"That's not true," I objected. "I just don't like all of the things you added for me." Although if Dad hadn't added the 'Do something different' to my hat, we wouldn't be sitting at the table right now. Did I wish I could take it all back? If I hadn't called Dominic, would we have started talking anyway? Would he have called me, or asked for help in class? Or would he have been gone before we got that far?

"I don't think we should get rid of the hats," I said slowly,

"Because I think Mom will promise never to do anything like this again. And I think we've all learned that it's okay to say yes."

*   *   *

Mom and Dad were still at the table, talking, but I had been excused. Grete was still happily watching the new Barbie movie.

I went to my room and looked at my bulletin board, staring at my list.

I need:
1) to be trusted
2) to be heard
3) to be believed
4) to be accepted for who I am; for my strengths
   and my weaknesses
5) to be given permission to fail
6) to be able to express myself
7) to be given reasonable responsibilities
8) to be given reasonable restrictions
9) to be able to be forgiven

I took the list off the board and added:

10) to be able to forgive

And I was pleased as I hung it back up. Ten was good number for a list, much better than nine.

Then I went to the computer.

I logged on to Facebook, and found a friend acceptance:
Dominic Martin has confirmed you as a friend.
And his personal message simply said, Sincerely.

S.L. Rottman is the award-winning author of many books for teens, including *Hero, Rough Waters, Stetson, Shadow of a Doubt, Slalom,* and *Out of the Blue.* A high school English teacher and avid reader, Rottman calls Colorado home.